WHEN SUMAC TURN RED

HARLAN FLICK

Lovstad Publishing
Baraboo, Wisconsin/Yuma, Arizona
Lovstadpublishing@gmail.com

WHEN SUMAC TURN RED
First Edition

ISBN:
ISBN-13: 9798730839311

Printed in the United States of America

Cover design by Lovstad Publishing
Sumac photograph by Pam Flick
Illustrations by Stacie Pliner

This book is dedicated to my brothers, Dale, Keith, Gordon, Russell, and Lester. As the youngest of five older brothers, I became the student, and they the teachers. I learned something from all of them, both individually, and collectively. They taught me to hunt and fish and to love and appreciate nature. They gave me a wonderful education, for which, I am forever grateful.

CONTENTS

WHEN
SUMAC
TURN
RED

WHEN SUMAC TURN RED

If you live in the Driftless Area, winter is the most unpleasant season of the year. Temperatures plummet, Canadian winds descend on the heartlands whipping at layered garments. Dry air cracks our skin forcing residents to apply enormous amounts of hand creams in a vain attempt to salvage our extremities. Residents barricade themselves in their houses, drink copious amounts of coffee, raid the refrigerator daily and discard their promise of eating no more than the 2,500 daily calories. A waning sun makes only a cameo appearance each day. Daylight, what little there is of it wanes quickly, a Houdini act that makes us believe in a dark magic.

Spring is wonderful when it finally arrives, but it is a fickle season with fits and starts. Just when you think spring has arrived another snowstorm comes along and dumps eight inches of white fairy dust to douse our enthusiasm. We watch the sun ascend a little higher in the sky each day, waiting patiently for the tapestry of wildflowers to push up through the permafrost and finally signal the arrival of spring.

Summer arrives in full force, a blast furnace of intolerance. Shorts and T-shirts are the uniforms of choice offering a respite from the heat and humidity that would otherwise engulf us. We laugh, play, and go to the beach as often as possible. We lather on sunscreen and wear floppy hats in a vain attempt to convince ourselves we are avoiding melanoma.

Summer ends abruptly making a crash landing over the Labor Day weekend. New clothes have been purchased, children scrubbed clean, as parents prepare to march their children off to begin another year of regimentation at school.

Winter, spring and summer close their chapters and await autumn's arrival. Autumn is everyone's favorite time of the year. There are few things that remind one more of the pending arrival of autumn than sumac shrubs. There are over 250 different varieties of sumac shrubs that populate the world. The U.S. alone has 35 varieties of flowering sumac.

The Latin name for sumac is Rhus glabra, "Rhus" meaning red. Most sumac have green compound leaves, but some have three leaflet leaves. The most common sumac in the Driftless Area are the Staghorn sumac and the smooth sumac.

Sumac are usually found in clusters near dry soil and rocky outcroppings where they serve a useful purpose. Once embedded they help maintain soil from erosion. As spring progresses, sumac spread by suckering, forming small thickets.

Some sumac is poisonous, but those are mostly located in Eastern Regions of the United States. Poison sumac have sparse leaves pointing upward. If your exposed skin encounters poison sumac, the leaves can cause a red, itching rash and blisters.

As the weather warms during the summer months flowers develop along with green and yellow berries. During the fall and winter months, the berries turn into clusters of green and white berries.

Birds such as gross beaks, northern cardinals, ruffed grouse, and partridges eat sumac berries in winter and early spring if the weather has turned particularly bitter and there are no other sources of food.

Native Americans used the shoots of sumac to make a type of salad. Jelly can be made from sumac as well as candy. It also can be made into tea and Jell-O. The leaves and bark of certain sumac can be made into dyes for tanning leather. The fruit from sumac is edible and is sometimes used for spices. Native Americans used the fruit from sumac as a sweetener.

As the summer sun finally begins to wane and the nights turn the Dog Days of summer to the more temperate evenings of September and October, plants and animals also go through their own vicissitudes. Plants slow their growth rate until they eventually stop growing. Animals pack on more weight as their fur grows longer. The excess fat and longer guard hairs give them a better chance of living through the upcoming months of bitter cold. Fish become aggressive in their feeding patterns, DNA triggering a feeding frenzy allowing fish to survive. They lose up to a thirty percent weight loss until ice melts in spring and plentiful food sources once again emerge. Fish move from the stronger currents of rivers and streams to slower moving water of lakes and backwater to preserve energy, lying dormant much of the time, conserving energy as they lie in darkness until the ice finally breaks up in March.

We do not often recognize the first signs of vicissitude in plants or animals. The late summer days and nights have not changed a great deal until someone in the local coffee shops says, "I had 35 degrees on my thermometer this morning."

Hunters soon get the urge to sight in their deer rifles, fishermen will turn their attention from catching pan fish to thoughts of catching fall pike. Duck hunters will spend more time working with their retrievers, tossing countless training dummies to their dogs in anticipation of the coming hunting season. Fly fishermen will tie larger flies, mostly hoppers and streamer patterns, in the hope of landing a hook-jawed brown trout ready to spawn, depositing their seed on the stream's bottom, enabling their species to survive.

It takes a while to recognize the cycle of life that is changing before us. One of the first signs of that change is the sumac shrub. It might be early September or just a few days later when someone first notices those changes. A local resident might be motoring along a country road, out for a leisurely drive through the countryside, when they first notice a clump of sumac scrubs. The motorist is almost past the sumac before they notice a slight difference in the coloration of the sumac leaves. Sumac leaves are often the first to change color and harbor in the first signs of autumn. The driver notices the red tint first, followed by a yellow coloration, and finally just a hint of orange. The driver slows his speed perceptively taking a closer look before fully realizing the sumac are changing color. The driver remains alert, their heart thrumming as they notice another clump of sumac whose vibrant colors strike a chord in their consciousness.

As nights cool, other trees will change the pigmentation of their leaves as well. Since the leaves of the sumac are the first to change color, they are also the first leaves to be denuded, their thin leaves scattering in the breeze creating an earthen carpet. Soon other trees will color and deposit their life's blood to the wind and rain of autumn.

For those of us who follow the ebb and flow of seasons in the Driftless Area, our hearts add a few beats per minute as we stop to gaze upon the splendor when sumac turn red.

HALF A PIKE

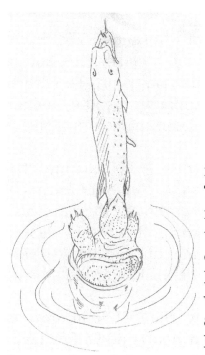

The joy of fishing did not infect Edy until later in life. There were three children to raise and an abusive husband to avoid. She never stepped outside her house when she had a black eye or any other visible sign of abuse. Bruised arms could be covered with long sleeves but bruises on her neck and face could not, so she simply stayed in the house and avoided people until the signs of abuse disappeared. She lived in a small Midwestern town where residents minded their own business and didn't interfere with the business of others. Even if they heard arguments and shouting, they would walk by quickly, eyes cast downward until they were past the altercation. It was an ingrained Midwestern belief that you simply did not interfere with what goes on with other families, and you didn't call the police. YOU JUST DIDN'T.

Edy's husband was a functional alcoholic. For all his bad habits which were many, he arose each day, drank several cups of strong coffee and trudged across the lawn to his garage 120 feet away.

His garage was a Quonset hut structure that was dark and smelled of spilled oil. The garage floor was stained, and a single light bulb hung precariously from

6

the ceiling. This single bulb was the only illumination he would have to do his daily work. He was an emotionally dark man who worked in a dark setting. He mostly did grunt work, changing oil, patching punctured tires, adding coolant in the summer and antifreeze to cars before the winter winds blew. His paycheck was an uneven affair that was dependent on how many customers he serviced. His was strictly a cash business. He might make reasonably good money one week and have few customers the next week. The inconsistency of a regular paycheck did nothing to improve his disposition. When anger overtook him, as it did on a frequent basis, it led to more liquor consumption. The liquor led to a downward spiral that was a harbinger to slapping, hitting, and choking. His wife was the easiest target and she took the brunt of his anger to shield her children from harm's way.

The three children, two girls and one boy, were not immune to his volcanic temper. The children avoided their father as much as they could, escaping to their bedrooms when the yelling started. They cowered in their rooms and covered their ears to be spared from the slapping and hitting that was about to commence.

He kept a bottle hidden in the garage and took nips throughout the day. He would sometimes go days without so much as a cross word to his wife or his children, but eventually his demons would descend upon him with a vengeance. It might be something as simple as dropping a wrench or stumbling over a tire he had forgotten to move out of the way. No one in his family could be sure when his temper might flare. They knew that it might happen at the most unexpected time so they were always on edge, afraid to speak loudly, or make any kind of a fuss that might set him off.

Edy tried as hard as she could to shield her children from their father, but their childhood was far from normal. Each stayed long enough to graduate High School but soon left the only home they had ever known to strike out in the world, wounded souls trying to forget where they were raised and what they had witnessed. They left their mother behind, not out of a lack of love, but out of a need for self-preservation. As they departed each child carried a certain amount of guilt, shame, and regret that their mother was left behind to fend for herself when all she had ever done was protect them. They wanted to help their mother, but they didn't know how, so they left and tried to save themselves.

Once the children were gone, Edy began to read articles about women who shared a similar background as herself, about life with an abusive husband. As she gained more knowledge about abuse, a sense of self-worth began to sprout and take root. It finally got to a point where she knew she had to get out of her marriage even though she was a devout Catholic.

She finally got up the courage to confront her husband and ask for a divorce. Her husband, oddly enough, gave only token resistance. He didn't raise his voice, nor did he threaten to hit her once he heard the news. A tear slid down his face and he simply nodded in agreement. He was getting older and each month left him with more aches and pains than the previous month. He was bone tired and had little fight left in him.

The divorce became final within a year. Edy got the house in the settlement but when her husband asked if he could move a tiny trailer onto the edge of their property, she couldn't bring herself to say no. The trailer was tiny. There was barely enough room inside for him to turn around. The trailer contained a small stove, a cramped bed, two chairs, a small closet, and a dish cabinet that contained three dishes, two glasses and one cup. He lived in that tiny trailer for four years, worked in his garage when his health allowed, and continued to drink daily until he finally died of alcohol poisoning.

He was buried on a Wednesday and Edy was the only one who showed up for his funeral. The three children all stayed away.

That first summer after her husband's death Edy planted a garden. She didn't know anything about gardening, but she soon found enjoyment turning over the earth, sifting the soil through her hands and breaking up large clumps of dirt with her fingers. When the soil was ready, she laid down a plumb line and planted seeds in straight, narrow rows. Once the seeds were planted, she waited for life to spring from the soil.

She found peace in gardening. There were no arguments, no one to tell her whether she was doing it right or wrong, and no one who would lay a hand on her.

She had few friends, none of whom she was particularly close to. She felt fine for the first time in years. She didn't mind being alone, but as time passed, she realized there was something missing in her life.

The answer to that question came on a warm summer day in June. She was working in her garden hoeing and weeding when she saw two young boys walking on the side of the road near her house. Both boys had fishing poles and they were carrying a stringer of fish. The boys were talking in an animated fashion obviously proud of their catch, hoping someone would take notice of their nice stringer of fish. She waved to the boys and they held up their catch which made her smile.

After the boys passed, she couldn't get the thought of how happy the boys looked with their fishing poles and the stringer of fish. Something had struck a chord with her and she couldn't stop smiling. She finally knew what she had been missing all these years. She needed a hobby, and she decided then and there that fishing was going to be that hobby.

The next week she went to a local auction on a whim not expecting to find anything worth buying. One of the last things up for sale was an old rod and reel. Most of the buyers had already left with their purchases when the bidding started. She bid five dollars for the rod and reel. No one else even bothered to make an offer which both surprised and pleased her at the same time.

The next day she worked in her garden much as she did every day. After she was done with her gardening, she took out the rod and reel and spent some time practicing casting.

She wasn't very good at casting and got backlashes on the reel more times than not, but with each passing day she improved. Within a week she proclaimed herself ready to go fishing for the first time in her life.

She went shopping at the local general store that sold a bit of everything and bought some hooks, split shot, a bobber and a metal stringer.

She spent the first official day of fishing under an overcast sky. She had dug some worms near the edge of her garden and put them in a Folgers coffee can. She walked a narrow-worn path that meandered toward the river. She tried avoiding the nettles and poison ivy as she walked along, and she kept a keen lookout for snakes. She only stopped once on her walk to smell a small cluster of wildflowers.

As she neared the river, she crossed a cement spillway that had a narrow wooden plank laid end to end. She looked down at the plank with trepidation, afraid to cross until she thought of all she has endured in her life. With that thought in mind, she took a tentative step and crossed the plank with a smile. When she got to the river, there was a wider spillway that had been built as part of the depression public works projects. The cement piers were sturdy structures, but most of the wood had deteriorated over the years due to weather and neglect. Two of the cement posts had several wide, wooden boards laid lengthwise. She crossed these with only mild trepidation and found a comfortable place to sit with her feet dangling over the water. She laid out her rod, the Folgers can containing the worms, and a small cloth sack that contained a sandwich, an apple, a jar of water, and a small cloth for cleaning her hands if she was lucky enough to catch a fish.

She baited a hook for the first time, impaling a fat worm on her hook that kept trying to wiggle free. She secured a bobber about four feet above the hook. She made a short cast and watched the worm disappear into the brown water of the Mississippi River.

She caught her very first fish that afternoon. She

saw the bobber move up and down before realizing she was supposed to set the hook. She jerked so hard the little sunfish came flying out of the water and landed in her lap. That little fish, too small to take home and eat, was solidly hooked, and so was she.

She spent three hours that day fishing and only caught three small fish. Most people would have given up after half an hour without a nibble and gone home. Edy, on the other hand, loved every minute she fished that day. There was no one to talk to which was just fine with her. She watched two ducks swim leisurely by and noticed a muskrat dive under water once it spied her perched on the wooden plank.

That night she took an old pair of men's trousers and used her scissors and sewing machine to modify them to fit. She rummaged through her closet until she found a faded shirt with long sleeves. She completed her fishing ensemble by commandeering her sun hat that she had been using for gardening.

The next morning, she was up early, eating a quick breakfast, before doing her gardening chores. Once those chores were done, she set off for the river. She settled into her spot on the wooden plank and from that point on time seemed to stand still. Nothing seemed to bother her, not the gnats that flitted around her eyes or the sun that beat down on her hands. For the first time in her life she was content and at peace with the world.

She caught four fish on her second outing, two large sunfish, a crappie and a small bass. She took the three larger fish home, scaled them, and fried them for her supper. She went to bed that night tired, but happy. By god, she thought, I am a fisher woman.

From that day forward Edy fell into a pattern, trying to fish every day unless it was raining, or she had some pressing business to attend to.

She fished well into the autumn. She watched the leaves turn color and drift into the river, little sail boats floating down stream. She gave up fishing in late November after frost covered the ground and ice crystals edged the shoreline.

She spent the next three years of her life fishing almost daily. During those years she became very adept at fishing. In early spring she caught fat perch filled with roe, their bellies so bloated it looked like they might burst. She filleted the perch, rolled the fillets in flour and dropped them into boiling oil until they were a crispy brown.

In summer she caught sunfish, crappies, and an occasional bullhead. Sometimes a large catfish would get hooked and her line would snap, too weak to hold the large fish.

She caught sheepshead and carp, saugers and skipjacks, suckers, bluegills and crappies. She once caught an ugly dogfish and she decided to cut the line rather than try to take the hook out. She caught a mudpuppy one day, a type of river salamander, and she chose to cut that line as well. She caught just about every type of fish in the river except for a walleye pike.

Every time she hooked into a large fish, she was sure it might be a walleye, but it never was. Catching a walleye became her obsession, day after day, week after week, month after month and year after year. She wasn't getting any younger and she knew she couldn't fish too many more years. She had arthritis in her joints, but she continued to fish day after day waiting for that one special day when a walleye might take a night crawler. If that day ever came, and the hook held, she would land the one fish that had for years evaded her.

She was fishing late in a lazy summer afternoon a few days after a thunderstorm had raised the water level in the river. It wasn't the best day to fish, the water high and brown. Her expectations weren't great after fishing for an hour without so much as a nibble. She looked away for a minute as she watched a turkey vulture circling overhead. When she eventually looked back, it took her a second to realize she could not locate her bobber.

Where did it go, she thought, where is my bobber? Her thoughts metastasized when she saw the line being stripped from her reel. She picked up her rod before it could tumble into the water, set the hook and began to fight the fish. She didn't know what kind of fish she had on, but she realized it was a very large fish. She didn't think it was a catfish because she knew catfish take out line in a zig zag pattern.

Could it be . . . was it possible . . . that this fish was a pike? Perhaps it was a northern pike. She had caught small northern pike before, but if this was a northern it was a big one.

She didn't want to get her hopes up that this fish was a walleye until she got it close to shore and saw it turn sideways in the water.

Once she saw the fish, she realized this was indeed a very large walleye. She reeled, the metal rod bent slightly, and the fish made another long run as it took out line.

The battle went on for several more minutes before

she could sense the fish was beginning to tire. Her hands were shaking so badly she wasn't sure she would be able to land the fish. She walked across the wooden plank and walked down a slight incline to get in a better position to land the pike. Finally, the walleye turned belly up and she was able to guide it into shallow water and pull it out onto a rock on the bank.

She got her metal fish stringer, passed it through the fishes' gills, went back to her wood plank and attached the stringer securely before dropping the stringer and the fish into the water.

It took her a few minutes before she could calm herself and stop shaking. She finally had caught the one fish that had eluded her. She was so happy she couldn't stop smiling.

She fished for another two hours, peaking every few minutes at the stringer that held her prize.

She was just about to leave when two sportsmen noticed her fishing and stopped by to ask if she had any luck.

She smiled broadly as she told the men about the fight with the fish. She said she was sure the pike would measure at least 24 inches long.

"Could we see the fish," one of the sportsmen asked?

"Oh, I'd be happy to show you my fish," she replied.

She started to pull up the metal stringer, but for some reason it was not coming up easily. There was a strong tug on the stringer before the fish began to rise out of the water. The head of the walleye emerged from the brown water but there was something dreadfully wrong because the walleye refused to come any farther.

Edy gave one more hard pull and the fish came half-way out of the water. The problem was only half the fish surfaced.

Attached to the fish was a huge snapping turtle. The turtle had devoured half of the walleye and was not giving up the other half without a fight. His jaws were clamped on the fish as he pulled the walleye under water.

Edy screamed, "My fish, my beautiful fish. What happened to my beautiful fish?"

Tears streamed down her face. She was inconsolable. She wept deep convulsive tears. Her whole body shook. She couldn't stand. She had to sit as her tears cascaded into the river, a small tsunami washing away her dream. Edy was inconsolable. She cried until she couldn't cry any longer.

The sportsmen tried to calm her, but she waved them off, too overcome to even speak.

She picked up her rod, left the stringer still tethered to her plank and walked home leaving the half pike to the turtle.

She never recovered from losing the pike.

She stayed in her house for another month before putting it up for sale.

She applied to an advertisement from an elderly couple in Madison. The couple was looking for a live-in care giver to meet their daily needs.

She moved to Madison a week after her house sold.

She lived with the elderly couple for five years. The husband died within two years and his wife passed away three years later. The elderly couple was wealthy, and they left Edy a small inheritance, enough to meet her basic needs for the rest of her life.

By happenstance, a neighbor from the small town Edy used to live in, ran into her on a street corner in Madison a short time later. The street was near Edy's small apartment. They went for coffee and chatted, but soon found little else to talk about. Their lives were now separated by years and after the conversation began to drag, they hugged and went their own way.

As the neighbor got up to leave, she remembered that Edy loved to fish.

"Edy, do you still fish," she asked?

"No," said Edy, "I haven't fished in years."

Edy passed away on a late spring day a few years later. Her three children and their four children came back for the funeral. They stayed on in Madison for a week to clear out her small apartment. They packed up clothes to give to Goodwill, took a few old photos for mementos and put up a sign advertising a yard sale to take place the next day.

There wasn't much to sell. There was a table and chairs, a set of dishes, a small dresser, an older television and other bits of odds and ends that people collect in their lifetime.

A man and his small son showed up just as the yard sale was finishing. There wasn't much left to sell. The only thing the man and his son noticed was an old rod and reel.

The man looked at his son who was nodding his head vigorously. The man said, "Would you take ten dollars for the rod and reel?"

"Sure, ten dollars would be fine," said Edy's son. "I don't know where it came from and it certainly isn't doing us any good."

THE WAYWARD BEAR

Wayward: Difficult to control. Willful. Turning away from what is normal or proper. Disobedient. Unpredictable. Erratic. Head strong.

If you have ever spent any time visiting and chatting with our neighboring residents from Canada, there is a fifty-fifty chance you will hear stories about black bears. Most of the stories will surround the mishaps Canadians have had with bears. The stories of Canadians and their encounters with black bears are ubiquitous. Once you have finished talking with our cousins to the north you are left with the belief that all Canadians have encountered a black bear at least once in their outings. Canadians' stories about black bears are as common as "Ole and Lena" jokes in Wisconsin. Wisconsinites it seems, spend half their lifetime memorizing Ole and Lena jokes and the other half of their lifetime retelling them.

Thank goodness there are no black bears in the driftless area of Wisconsin.

Do not get me wrong, there are plenty of black bears in Wisconsin. The good folks of Wisconsin agree there are thousands of black Bears in the upper third of the state and they agree that is where the bears should stay. "But," they will say, "black bears do not inhabit the lower, driftless area of the state."

"There ain't no black bears here," they will say. "If you want to shoot a black bear, you gotta go north."

The black bears inhabit large northern forested areas and swampland where they forage on grass, roots, berries, insects, fish, mammals, human foods from garbage dumps and tipped over trash bins. Black bears are not discriminatory when it comes to eating. They eat what is available, whenever it is available.

Male black bears are generally 47 to 70 inches long and weigh, on average, 250 to 300 pounds. Male black bears can, however, weigh as much as 700 to 800 pounds.

Our northern brethren often have encounters with black bears, and much like their Canadian cousins are not particularly spooked when they happen to meet up with a bear. The great majority of those encounters are benign with the bears taking a hasty retreat once they smell or see a human.

Those of us who live in the southwestern quadrant of the state, have likely never seen a bear in the wild. Our only encounter with a black bear is when the bear is looking through metal bars from an enclosure in a zoo. That is simply fine with us. Truth be told, we have a real fear of black bears. We've heard stories of bears attacking people and our ignorance of bears only heightens our distrust of them.

Black bears, on rare occasions, will attack humans. Black bears have killed 63 people in the last 109 years. Black bear attacks are more common than grizzly bear attacks simply because of the sheer number of black bears compared to the number of grizzlies. Grizzly bears are twenty times more dangerous than black bears. You are more likely to die from a bee sting than being killed by a black bear. In those rare occasions when an attack does occur, black bears might maim, bite, and claw, but the victim almost never dies. That doesn't give the good folks who live in the driftless area a great deal of confidence, so it is a great relief to those of us who call the driftless area of Wisconsin home that there are no black bears where we live. We sleep well at night with the knowledge we will not encounter any black bears.

Those of us who have lived in the driftless area for many years have seen several changes that have affected our lives and changed the region. We used to have large numbers of red foxes and no coyotes. About three decades ago that slowly started to change. Coyotes started traveling south and we began to hear their yapping as the sun went down. Now we have an abundance of coyotes, some of them living in urban areas, while most of the red foxes have fled the country or been killed by the encroaching coyotes. We have seen changes over the past several decades but thank goodness we have not seen any black bears where we live.

If you read the brochures about bear encounters

with humans, the sage advice is to stay calm and talk in a gentle voice. Do not run. The brochures always encourage hunters and fishermen to carry bear spray, which is a type of pepper spray. If a bear charges, wait until the bear is within thirty feet before discharging the spray. Do not aim the bear spray at the head of the bear. Aim the spray at the feet of the bear. The spray will rise quickly giving you a better chance of the spray hitting the bear in the eyes.

Here is the part of the story where I tell you the bad news. The Department of Natural Resources estimates there are between 24,000 to 28,000 black bears in the state. Several years ago, the DNR admitted they had underestimated the black bear population in Wisconsin by a factor of .... SEVEN. The bear population in the state has exploded.

That brings us to the journey of one exceptionally large black bear. He is not an 800 pounder, but he is a very heavy bodied bear. One day, for reasons we do not fully understand, that bear decided to go on a walkabout. He wandered a bit not heading in any specific direction, eating mostly grass and digging up roots and occasionally finding grubs which offered a source of protein. As he grazed throughout the late afternoon hours, he gradually started to head in a southerly direction. He did not necessarily make this choice consciously. Maybe the food was plentiful, so he was content to keep on grazing in the direction he was headed. Perhaps he had been pushed out by the excess number of bears in the north. Maybe, as the song says, he was, "looking for love in all the wrong places," and he thought his prospects would be better served by heading south.

We may never know the answer to those questions, but for whatever reason, the black bear kept moving south. Black bears are incredibly good climbers. The large bear would spend his days in an oak tree or a hollowed-out log sleeping away most of the daylight hours. He would climb down from the tree in late afternoon and begin foraging. The tree had offered protection and the large oak leaves offered camouflage. It takes a lot of food to satisfy a 500-pound bear. Once on the ground the bear would turn over rocks, use his huge paws to rip apart rotten logs looking for insects, and dig for roots and tubers. He needed water daily and his sensitive nose could smell a spring, creek, or field pond from miles away. If the pond were large enough, he would take a cooling swim before getting out, shaking off his thick coat and continuing his way southward. He avoided towns and people whenever possible and that is one of the reasons he slept most of the day.

The bear was not in a hurry. If food were readily available, he would stay in an area until the food supply dwindled. He particularly loved berries and would devour blackberries and wild strawberries until they were all gone. He deposited his scat where it fell and birds picked through the scat for seeds, passing it through their systems and created new berry patches in the process.

As days passed the bear continued south. One day the bear caught the scent of an animal carcass ten miles away. It took him a good portion of the day to cover the ten miles, foraging as he went until he came upon the deer carcass. The deer had been dead for some time and smelled accordingly. The smell made no difference to the bear who fed upon the carcass until he had consumed twenty pounds of venison. He covered the deer carcass with debris to keep scavengers at bay before finding a large tree and climbing to the safety of a notch high in the branches. He closed his eyes and slept.

He stayed with the deer carcass for three days, protecting it from scavengers. He gorged himself on the deer and left only after the bones had been picked clean.

Each day was a carbon copy of the day before. The bear continued heading in a southern direction. When food was plentiful, he moved slowly. When food was scarce, the bear quickened his pace.

The terrain was beginning to change. Hard wood forests were replacing pines. There was plenty of water available when he was thirsty and enough food to meet his needs, so he felt no urgency to change the direction he had been following. He avoided towns and dogs unless they were tied or in a kennel. Somehow, he knew dogs could not follow him if they couldn't get off a chain or out of a kennel.

He could smell town dumps from a great distance. He waited until darkness before exploring a dump site. A dump, to a bear, is like a buffet restaurant. It is an all you can eat smorgasbord. The bear could pick and choose what he ate and often chose food that had a sweet flavor. If he heard a garbage truck approach he would slink back into the undergrowth and wait until the garbage had been deposited, then wait another hour before he came out to gorge himself on the new deposits of food.

He often smelled humans and would find a

convenient place to hide in a tree. His eyesight was not particularly good, and he could not distinguish the large form of a human from further than thirty yards away. He depended on his nose for protection and when he smelled humans, he turned and sought to distance himself from their smell.

He entered the southwestern part of Wisconsin in early July. He was in the driftless area now and began to adapt to the high bluffs and limestone outcroppings. He had not encountered another bear in many weeks. July is the normal time for black bears to mate. If he was looking for a female to breed, he was out of luck. He wandered the deep woods in late afternoons as shadows were cast across the landscape. He tested the air every few minutes for the smell of a female bear in heat, but he neither smelled nor saw a likely mate.

He explored this new terrain attempting to put his claim on this new territory. Autumn would be coming soon, and with that colder weather. Before long he would have to start searching for a den before cold weather set in, but that could wait for the time being. There were small creeks nearby and field ponds were common, so he never had to travel any great distance for water.

The terrain suited him fine. The high bluffs gave him cover and the hardwood forests offered large trees where he could sleep away most of the day. He would climb down from his perch in the tree in late afternoon and start searching for food and water. He sometimes awoke earlier in the day and climbed down when hunger pangs woke him up. One day flowed into the next and the bear soon became comfortable with his surroundings. He had heard dogs barking from time to time, but they never seemed to venture into the forest. He had traveled a long way over many days and was content to stay where he was and travel no further. He continued to sniff the air each day in hopes of smelling a female bear in heat not realizing he had ended his journey in an area where there were no other bears.

The sun's assent and decent across the sky shortened a bit every few days and the weather had turned cooler at night. The bear remained healthy after his long journey, and he began consuming more calories each week, some genetic barometer telling him to eat as much as possible so he could survive the onslaught of winter. The bear didn't realize it, but his days of remaining an invisible figure in the forest were rapidly coming to an end. Two local farmers whose farms adjoined one another were the first to see the bear. They would see the bear near dusk at the edge of their fields as he turned over sod with his great claws looking for ants and grubs. They were not particularly happy that their fields were being uprooted but they kept their knowledge of the bear to themselves. Neither of them had ever seen a black bear in the wild before and after discussing the matter at some length, decided they would keep the secret of the bear to themselves. They would look out over their fields each afternoon in the hope of spotting the bear. Most days the bear never materialized, but on those days when he did slip out of the forest undetected the farmers enjoyed the privileged of being able to watch him forage for food. If the bear left their milk cows alone, which so far he had, the farmers were happy to keep the bear their secret and were content to watch the bear from afar.

More weeks passed and the nights cooled. There was frost on the ground most mornings. Leaves had turned brilliant colors, and people said the fall foliage was one of the most beautiful years in recent memory due to cool nights and bright sunny days. Folks seemed to be in a festive mood as traffic picked up on rural highways. City folks were flocking to the countryside to see the fall colors, stopping often to snap photos and have a picnic lunch. There were oohs and ahs, as spectators watched leaves fluttering in the breeze, releasing their final grip on branches as gravitational pull sent them tumbling to the ground with every breeze, a multicolored snowstorm lighting up the landscape.

Mike Phillips parked his pickup on his 60-acre parcel of land on a crisp mid-October morning. He carried his Mathews bow and three carbon tipped arrows along with a thermos of coffee and a sack lunch of two bologna sandwiches, three apples, and eight miniature Milky Way candy bars. He climbed a steep hill and soon began to perspire from the exertion before he got to his tree stand that overlooked a field pond. He did not expect to shoot a deer on this beautiful fall day unless a trophy buck happened to be particularly thirsty and moseyed down to take a drink.

Mike had the itch to get out of the house, set his butt on a tree stand, and watch the beauty of nature unfold before him. He had complete confidence he would still shoot at least two deer during the bow and gun seasons. The reason for that confidence was embedded in the fact that he accomplished that goal every year for the past nine years.

Mike had settled into his seat on the tree stand and

started scanning the deer trail that was ten yards from where he was perched twenty-five feet off the ground. Two chipmunks soon came out to play, scampering across logs in a game of tag. Mike watched the chipmunks for fifteen minutes until they scampered off, as he became distracted by the cawing of two crows who had landed in a nearby tree.

It was at that moment when Mike first saw the bear. He turned from the crows and looked directly at the bear who was about thirty yards away. He had to look a second time to assure himself his eyes were not playing tricks on him. Mike had never seen a bear in the wild before and the sight of the bear shook him to his core. The bear seemed oblivious to the man in the tree. The bear raised his head every few steps to sniff the air. The bear was not in a hurry but was headed directly toward Mike's tree stand. Mike did not know whether to yell at the bear to scare it away or allow the bear to pass close to his stand in the hope the bear wouldn't know Mike was in the tree. In the end, Mike was too nervous to do either of those things. The bear was much closer now and was looking directly at Mike perched in the tree.

The bear stood under Mike's tree for a moment, tested the air with his nostrils, stood on his hind legs, extended his paws up the tree trunk and began to climb.

Mike's brain was in overdrive. Should he shoot the bear as it climbed the tree or yell at the bear? His brain was processing information at warp speed when he remembered seeing the bear testing the air. Maybe the bear was hungry, had smelled Mike's food and decided to come and get it. Mike did not want to shoot the bear so he grabbed his lunch and pulled out an apple and threw it at the bear. The apple ricocheted off the bears muzzle and landed under the tree. The bear descended the tree, picked up the apple with his mouth and ate it. Once the bear was done with the apple, he again started to climb the tree. Mike threw another apple at the bear, who once again climbed down the tree to eat the apple.

Mike knew this standoff with the bear could not last forever because the bear did not appear to be going anywhere. Mike took out his bologna sandwich and threw it as far from the tree as he could. The bear lumbered over and picked up the sandwich and made short work of it. Mike threw the last sandwich to distract the bear, but the bear slowly walked over and ate that sandwich as well.

Mike, who had been a pitcher of limited ability in high school, picked up the last apple, wound up and threw the apple as far as his super-charged adrenaline would allow. As the bear slowly meandered toward the apple, Mike gathered up his gear and what was left of his lunch and quickly climbed out of the tree. Mike started to walk at a fast pace downhill towards his vehicle, but when he looked back, the bear had devoured the apple and was following him.

Mike took one of the miniature Milky Way candy bars and dropped it as he kept walking. The bear tore part of the wrapper off the candy bar before eating it. Mike kept walking as the bear came closer, before dropping another Milky Way bar. He continued doing this until he dropped the last Milky Way bar just before reaching his vehicle. He was so nervous about the encounter with the bear that he dropped his keys twice before unlocking the car.

Mike went home and told his wife about the encounter with the bear, but he did not tell anyone else. He was embarrassed about how nervous he was when the bear started to climb the tree he was in. He had never gotten that nervous while aiming at a trophy buck, but the bear, he admitted to himself, had spooked him.

Three weeks later, Dan Fenske and Bill Fowler entered a nearby section of farmland they had recently leased for hunting deer. Neither was an experienced hunter, but both had expensive hunting rifles. Since they were inexperienced hunters, they decided they should hunt close together. They set up makeshift blinds behind discarded tree limbs. They had spent most of the day looking at an empty forest without so much as sighting a deer. The shadows were deepening as the sun started to dip on the horizon. Dan saw the bear first and tried to quickly dial Bill's phone, but he was so nervous he dropped his phone once and misdialed twice before Bill picked up. Bill came running from his blind and both men started out of the woods while keeping an eye on the bear that seemed to be following them.

The farmer who had leased the land to the hunters watched as the two men walked backwards out of the woods. "Why are you fellas walking backwards? You look like you've seen a ghost."

"It, it wasn't no ghost," stammered Bill. "It was a damn bear, a monster bear."

Both men were shaking badly. The farmer, who had seen the bear numerous times over the summer and early fall, was a bit embarrassed and finally confessed he had seen the bear numerous times.

"This is a helluva time to tell us now," said Dan. "We want our money back. We didn't lease your land so a damn bear could attack us."

"That bear hasn't bothered no one," said the farmer.

"We are out of here and we aren't coming back. You will be hearing from our lawyer about that lease we signed. You never told us you had a bear on the property. That bear scared the hell out of us. We are contacting the DNR to come and shoot that bear."

With that, they climbed in their car and spewed gravel as they sped out of the farmer's driveway.

Three days later two Wisconsin game wardens came to the farmer's house and questioned him about the hunter's complaint. They took the farmer's statement and he admitted there was a bear in the area, and the bear had forced the two hunters to back out of the woods while keeping an eye out for the bear.

"What's going to happen to the bear," asked the farmer? "We never had a bear around here before and we kind of enjoy seeing him. He is almost like a pet. We don't want to see him shot."

The two wardens excused themselves to talk privately for a few minutes. After a short discussion, the wardens returned to talk to the farmer once again.

"We wish you would have called us as soon as you saw the bear this summer. It is probably a lone bear looking for his own territory, but it is not a good situation when a bear gets too used to humans. We will talk to our supervisor and our best guess is we will try to catch the bear in a live trap or shoot him with a tranquilizer gun. If we can accomplish either one of those scenarios, we will be able to relocate the bear farther north."

"And if you can't trap the bear?"

"If we can't capture the bear, we will have to find him and euthanize him."

"You mean, kill him?"

"Ya, unfortunately we would have to put him down."

"People around here just aren't used to bears and they don't know how to deal with them."

With that, the two wardens got back in their car and drove away. They would be back in a few days, with a decision made by a superior living a few hundred miles away.

We have lived through an invasion of coyotes in the past thirty years. We have ticks that now carry Lyme disease, bobcats are being spotted throughout the region in recent years, deer now die from blue tongue (EHD, a viral disease) caused by gnats. We have tested for Chronic Wasting Disease for years now. Nature changes and we have no choice, but to adapt with it.

If you go in the woods, it might now be advisable to carry bear spray with you. If more black bears do move into the Driftless Area, we will adjust to them just as folks in the northern third of the state have many years ago.

If you do not want to carry bear spray, maybe you should carry some apples and a few Milky Way candy bars, just to be on the safe side.

THE LAST COON DOG TRIALS

If you grew up in the Heartland of America, particularly if it was the Driftless region that encompasses parts of Minnesota, Iowa, and Wisconsin, you should consider yourself lucky. Chances are you probably grew up in a small town. There are not many big cities in the Driftless Region. Some might consider Minneapolis-St. Paul, Milwaukee and Iowa City as metropolitan areas, but that is about it. What the Driftless area lacked in large cities with shopping malls, restaurants, and entertainment centers was balanced by thousands of small towns ranging in size from a few hundred citizens to tiny hamlets of only a handful of houses and a few inhabitants. Most of the residents in these small towns thought they had the better lifestyle.

On the outskirts of most small towns lay fertile farmland. Families who lived and toiled on those farms milked thirty or forty cows twice a day and raised cash crops of corn, soybeans, and wheat. Some farmers in southwest Wisconsin raised tobacco. A farmer could make good money raising tobacco, but it helped if they had numerous children to assist with planting, cultivating, and topping the tobacco. Harvesting tobacco normally took place in early September. The tobacco crop was then put on laths and hung in tobacco sheds to cure. The tobacco was taken down later and the leaves stripped on foggy nights in November and December. Many farmers loved raising tobacco for the extra money it brought in, but their children who had to do much of the back-breaking work generally hated it.

The residents of small towns had to hustle to find jobs that paid a living wage. Many of them were willing to drive thirty or forty miles one way to secure such a job. Unfortunately, those jobs were few and far between and the competition to land such a job was intense.

Most who had made the choice to live in the Driftless Area did so because they fell in love with the natural beauty that glaciers never touched. The high bluffs that overlooked verdant valleys and meandering streams were a siren's call they found powerless to resist. It spoke to them, "this is home." They loved the proximity to the Mississippi River where they could fish and hunt for both small and large game. The hard wood forests provided an abundance of deer, squirrels, grouse, and rabbits that the locals enjoyed hunting each year. When wild turkeys were successfully reintroduced to the state, it provided yet another confirmation they had made the right choice of a place to call home.

The picture painted of small towns and its rural residents was a life lived around natural beauty. This was a place they chose to live and raise their families with the economic realities that reminded them daily their chances of growing economically prosperous were slim at best. Most concluded the quality of life the region had to offer was worth more than a higher paycheck.

There were months when families barely made enough money to pay the bills. When you are self-employed, there is no guaranteed paycheck. Milk prices fluctuated and beef prices were variable as well. Most small dairy operations scraped by as farmers working twelve to fifteen-hour days, seven days a week. With those kind of work schedules, it certainly did not leave much time for entertainment. Farmers got their milk checks on Friday. That was the day the family drove to town to cash the check. They would stop at the general store for groceries and other necessary supplies for the farm.

There were free movies shown on an outdoor screen. The screen was often just a white sheet stretched between two poles. About the only other opportunity for entertainment might be a family outing to the Mississippi River to fish, or a trip to the local swimming hole so kids could splash in the warmth of a pond. Even these were rare occasions because farm work never ceased.

To help supplement their income and as a way of putting a few more dollars in the Mason jar, farmers might do custom work for neighboring farmers or help harvest another acre of back breaking, but cash generating, tobacco.

A few farmers had coon dogs and would hunt raccoon in the fall after their farm chores were done.

Most farmers had no fondness for raccoon because the little masked bandits raided their corn fields and knocked over corn stocks. The farmers who found enough energy to hunt raccoon for a few hours each evening, enjoyed the paycheck when they sold the coon pelts to the local fur buyer.

Few farmers had the inclination or the time to hunt raccoon after a back breaking day doing chores from sunup to sundown, so it was mostly the residents of small hamlets who raised and hunted coon dogs. A man could make some extra spending money if he had one or two good coon hounds. If coon pelt prices spiked, which typically occurred later in the season when the hides were prime with thick fur, you would see a welcome increase of a few dollars. A good coon hide could bring a hunter five or six dollars in the 1950's and sixties. If you had a couple good hounds, you might get four to six coon a night. If you were lucky, you might get more than that. Hunting coon, of course, was dependent on the quality of the hunting dogs and the weather. If it rained when you were out hunting, the dogs would lose the scent of the raccoon. When it was extremely dry, the dogs couldn't follow the scent that the coon gave off.

In addition to the extra cash the hunter received for the coon pelts, what coon hunters enjoyed most was listening to the dogs work out a track. A hound would let out a howl when they smelled the track of a raccoon and the chase would commence. If the dogs treed a raccoon, the hunter would hustle to the dogs and spot the raccoon in the tree with a flashlight. Once the coon was spotted, you used your .22 to shoot the raccoon out of the tree. If the raccoon had scampered up an oak tree, the hunter might not be able to spot the masked critter even with a good light. The coon would hide in the thick oak leaves and the hunter could spend half an hour shining his light over the tree and never see the coon. The hunter would have wasted thirty minutes before he had to pull the coon dogs off the tree. In addition to the wasted time looking for the raccoon in the tree, the dogs constant bellowing would have chased away any raccoon who had been in the area. The hunter would have to call the dogs off the tree and send them out to find another fresh coon track.

There were two brothers in Iowa who farmed all day and hunted coon most of the night. They would alternate nights, one brother going out one night and the other brother hunting the next. Between the two brothers they would kill more than two hundred raccoon during the season. They owned two big, raw boned red tick hounds that came from a good blood line. The brothers lived in a heavily wooded area where no one else bothered to hunt raccoon. They made good money hunting coon with their top-of-the-line hounds, but they had to get by with little sleep during the hunting season and still get up in the morning to run a large farm.

There was one event that occurred each summer that appealed to those looking for free entertainment and those who had coon hounds. In the 1950's through the early 1980's people would gather for the annual Coon Dog Trials. The trials always took place outside a small unincorporated village. It was a rural area made up of small farms sandwiched between high bluffs.

One of the local farmers rented out a small section of his land for the one-day event. The trials always took place on a weekend which guaranteed a large crowd of spectators. Posters advertising the trials had been displayed for a few weeks prior to the event. The advertising brought out people who had never seen an event like this before. It was not just local folks who showed up. People came from surrounding towns and cities when they learned this wasn't just another small-town event but rather, a spectacle. On the morning of the trials, pickup trucks started pouring into the event location. The pickups would trample the grass, and tents or tarps would be erected for shade. Coon hounds who seemed to sense what was going on would be tied to any shrub or tree that was available, before being watered and fed.

Hounds, by nature like to howl. As more pickups showed up, containing even more hounds, the howls started to reverberate throughout the valley. This only added to the festive nature of the day. The newcomers had their own dogs to be watered, fed, and tethered. There was always someone who showed up with hound pups for sale. Negotiation would start and if a fair price could be agreed upon, the pup would go home with a new owner.

This was a special day for hound owners, hunters, townspeople, and especially for onlookers who had never seen anything like this before. It was a day that was part carnival, part gambling day, and most important of all, one large beer party. The weather was almost always hot and humid, and the gathering crowd soon wanted to quench their thirst. Cold beer flowed early and often, tongues loosened up and stories were swapped. As the day continued to unfold many of the spectators ended up, as the locals would say,

'Three sheets to the wind.' There was a lot of drinking, a lot of vomiting, and a lot of spectators who became very, very drunk.

The coon dog trials were a contest to see which dog would be the first to follow a coon trail and tree a raccoon. A few men would take a coon hide, douse water on the pelt to produce greater amounts of coon scent for the dogs to follow. The hide was then dragged over a set course, through woods, around bushes and over barren ground. The coon hide was eventually dragged to a designated tree and rubbed against the trunk of the tree. A live raccoon had already been hoisted up into the tree in a wire mesh basket. The basket was tied to a tree limb. There was an exceptionally large painted circle around the bottom of the tree. Once the trail had been laid, the festivities were ready to begin.

A local auctioneer would gather everyone in a large circle and the betting would begin. Each dog owner brought their dog forward for their race. There were several ways a dog could win money for their owner. The first dog to finish the race by entering the circle below the tree would be assured of winning part of the purse. The second dog to finish in the circle would win a lesser amount of money for its owner. The first dog to enter the circle and bark at the coon up in the tree would win part of the purse as would the second dog who barked at the treed coon.

The purse for the race was determined by those who made bets on the dogs who were entered in any given race. The dogs in any upcoming race were brought out and anyone who wished to bet on a race would step forward and the bidding would commence.

Anyone could bet on any dog in any given category. Locals who came to the coon dog trials each year had a bit of an advantage. They remembered the winning dogs from previous years. They would bid those dogs up higher because they felt those dogs had a better chance of winning or placing. The bidding was like any auction. Beauty was in the eye of the beholder. There were dogs that garnered a higher bid simply because they were nice looking dogs. Looks, however, can be deceiving and bidders were often disappointed when some mediocre looking dog got a place and won some money for its owner.

The bidding was fast and furious. Like most auctions, bidders could get into a bidding war with several people determined to out-bid the other. There were large amounts of money in the kitty when the last dog had been auctioned off. The owners who entered one of their dogs in a race had to pay an entry fee, so owners had skin in the game as well. The entry fee money went into the kitty, which often grew into hundreds of dollars. Owners could bet on their own dogs as well.

After the bidding was done, the dogs were led to the starting line by their owners. The owners were stroking their hounds, talking to them, getting them pumped up for the big race. A gun was fired off as the dogs shot off the starting line, the coon scent fresh in their nostrils, the hounds bellowing, jostling for position. The race usually lasted around ten minutes. The spectators could hear the bellowing of the hounds at the start of the race and again near the end of the race. The spectators were held back by a roped off area near the tree that housed the raccoon. Spectators would cheer on the dogs whether they had bet on them or not. The excitement of the race was contagious as the hounds bellowed and the money gambled on the dogs only heightened the spectator's fervor.

After a few short minutes, the first dog would enter the viewing area and the spectators would erupt with cheers. Other dogs were only a short distance behind as they tried to separate themselves from the rest of the pack. The finish was always close and not without controversy. There might be three or four dogs around the tree before one of the dogs barked at the coon in the tree. Three other dogs might start to bark almost simultaneously after the first dog claimed the top spot. The owners of the other three dogs thought it was their dog that was the second to bark at the coon in the tree therefore earning that owner part of the purse. Arguments were common among owners, with each arguing for their dog and against other dogs. It was common for dog owners to start cussing at one another. "Goddammit, my dog was second to tree you sonuvabitch. Everybody seen it."

The language at coon dog trials wasn't for the feint of heart.

There were judges who had the final say in disputes, but grudges lasted, and fights were not unheard of. Every owner wanted their share of the pot and hard feelings festered when someone thought their dog had been robbed of a rightful place.

Coon hunters are a hearty breed and often cantankerous by nature. They are a tough lot not inclined to give an inch when it comes to a good argument. Plus, they had money on the line. There were travel expenses, entry fees to pay and there was no guarantee of winning any part of the purse. As the day went on tempers got shorter, not helped by the beer that was being consumed and purse money won or lost.

There was one raw boned guy who showed up every year for the trials. He was about six-four and well over 200 pounds. He was a well-built guy with long stringy hair. If you came to the trials on a regular basis you would recognize him easily enough because he wore a big Bowie knife in a sheath on his belt. Every year the guy seemed to get under the skin of someone. He would get into a heated argument and about the time blows were to reign down on someone smaller than him, he would say loud enough for all to hear, "My hands are registered with the U.S. military. I've been trained in the U.S. Army. I'd fight you, but I'd get in trouble with the law."

The next year the same guy would show up and the same scenario would repeat itself until he staggered off looking for another beer. I guess you would say he was all bark and no bite.

There was a man from Iowa who came each year with two black and tan coon hounds. It did not take many years of attending the event before his dogs became the preferred betting favorites. Local men who knew the reputation of his dogs would say, "When is that feller from Iowa going to get here? Them dogs of his is always fit as a fiddle, and by god, they win more times than not."

Once the Iowa man brought his hounds into the bidding circle the crowd of bidders suddenly became much larger and his dogs always brought the highest bids. It was not unusual for his coon dogs to be first in the circle and first to bark at the coon in the tree. He never entered both of his dogs in the same race. He would split the dogs up in separate races and often win races with each dog.

At the end of the day, he pocketed more prize money than anyone else. His were real coon hounds who hunted coon every night of the season, weather permitting. The coon dog trials were just another way for the Iowa man to make some extra money.

The trials started in the morning and lasted until late afternoon. By late in the day, most spectators had bad sun burns and were a little tipsy from too many brews. When the final race was run, the dogs were loaded back in the trucks and a few spectators went home with a hound pup they had not owned when they arrived that morning. Preparations for the next summer's trials were loosely discussed before everyone loaded up their vehicles and headed for home.

By the time the sun was setting the trial site was a mess. Grass that had been tall and green that morning had been thoroughly trampled. There were beer bottles strewn throughout the premises. The farmer, whose land the trials were held on would come in the next day and clean up the debris. The farmer would receive a few hundred dollars for the one-day use of his land.

Everyone thought the trials would go on year after year. The public enjoyed it, the farmer and some of the dog owners made a little extra money. The spectators had a good excuse to spend some of their hard-earned cash and an opportunity to drink a few too many beers.

Two events ended the coon dog trials in the early 1980's and left them on the scrapheap of small-town life. The first event seemed simple enough that no one saw it coming. Any dog could be brought to the coon dog trials. There were no regulations on the breed of dogs that could be entered. The trials went on year after year with coon hounds until one year a guy shows up with some greyhounds. Although greyhounds are technically hounds, most people saw them as an exotic breed known for their speed. They were sight hunters, preferring to see their prey rather than using their noses to follow it. Most folks did not think much of these sleek, skinny dogs with long snouts and skinny legs.

Two greyhounds were entered into a race a few years later. They had not been bid up very high during the auction. Most spectators did not give them much of a chance against the coon hounds. When the starting gun went off the greyhounds stayed back in the pack. They were loping along content to stay with the pack and let the hounds follow the sent. That all changed once the race was nearly over. Once the greyhounds sighted the crowd of spectators, they hit another gear and left the hounds far behind. The two greyhounds came in first and second to the tree. Greyhounds are pretty much a silent breed. Their bark is more like a whimper, so all hell broke out when a greyhound let out a small whimper and its owner declared the dog to be first to bark at the coon in the tree. Just about that time the hounds came in and two of them barked at the tree right away. An argument ensued between the coon hound owners and the greyhound owner. A meeting of officials took place and after a long discussion their ruling was that the greyhound, even with its small whimper was declared the first to bark at the tree.

The Iowa man was there with his two prized black and tan hounds, but even his prized hounds could not begin to keep up with the greyhounds. The coon dog trials that year ended in hard feelings on all sides. Those hard feeling continued the next few summers when fewer hounds were entered in races and more Greyhounds won a greater share of the races and prize money.

The coon dog trials finally ended some years later not because of the conflicts between coon dog owners versus greyhound owners, but because of an organization that was just beginning to flex its political might. PETA, People for the Ethical Treatment of Animals, was established on March 22, 1980. The organization whose tenant was the ethical treatment of animals sued against the treatment of the raccoon that was in a cage in the tree. The raccoon, they reasoned, was traumatized by the baying of the hounds under the tree. This did not go over well with the hound owners or the greyhound crowd. Eventually, PETA changed everything, and the coon dog trials gradually died out as PETA lawsuits multiplied.

It has been almost forty years since coon dog trials came to an end. Society, for the most part, gradually accepted the changes. Coon Dog Trials became a thing of the past and slipped from our collective consciousness except for old timers who remember the joy of Coon Dog Trials from a bygone era.

"Hell," they would say, "it's a damn coon. They get killed by cars in the thousands every summer. The coon knocks down farmers corn stocks and eat their corn. You think PETA is going to pay those farmers for their lost crops? By god, what is the world coming to when you protect a damn coon? That damn organization made us stop having Coon Dog Trials which was the highlight of the summer for a lot of us. I don't know what the hell the world is coming to when one coon can stop a tradition that never hurt anyone, including the coon."

Coon Dog Trials gradually slipped into the history of small-town life. As time passed, fewer and fewer hunters even bothered to hunt coon. It became much more common for landowners to post their land with no trespassing signs, so hunting coon became problematic. PETA even started protesting the use of fur on coats, gloves and wraps. A flourishing fur industry has pretty much dried up. The price of coon pelts plummeted, and a way of life changed in rural communities. What was once a celebration of hunting and comradery, became nothing but a distant memory when dogs would bray, men would wager, and one lonely coon would peer down from its perch in a tree.

A DEER KILLING

Harry "Bub" Franklin stood on a knoll to rest his bad knee before walking further. He removed his red and black checkered hat. The hat, sun faded and sweat stained, contained flaps that would cover his ears when the late afternoon temperature plummeted. The flaps were tethered on the top of the hat with string bindings now because he was sweating from the climb. His heavy jacket matched the color of the hat. The regulations making these colors mandatory was enacted in 1945. The regulations stated that half of a hunters outer clothing had to be of predominantly red material.

He wiped perspiration from his brow with the hat and thought about all the years he had hunted deer. He considered how much he had learned of deer habits and how much he knew about the history of deer hunting in Wisconsin. He was, by local standards, an encyclopedia of information on deer and deer hunting. It was his avocation to study old laws about hunting deer in his native state. He scoured old documents to learn as much as he could about old-time hunts and their effect on hunting regulations in Wisconsin. Regulations were never set in stone and they continued to periodically change over time.

He was a human resource of historical information and would regale anyone who cared to listen, and some who didn't, about the long history of Wisconsin deer hunting. Wisconsin had deer hunting regulations that dated back to 1851 and Bub made it his mission to understand each addition and subtraction of those regulations. Hunting deer was his passion and knowing the history of hunting deer In Wisconsin was his avocation.

Did anyone other than Bub know, or even care to know, that the first reports of crop damage by deer was reported in 1834? The 1851 deer season closed February 1 and remained closed until June 30. Native Americans, however, could hunt year-round.

There was a law passed in 1892 that made it lawful to kill any dog found running deer. By 1899 the limit was two deer per season and the cost of a resident license was one dollar. By 1909 the season had been shortened to twenty days. In 1915, the state declared the first buck only deer season.

In 1917, shining deer became illegal for the first time. In 1925, deer season was only open in alternate years. In 1934, the first archery season was enacted. By 1941, there were few deer predators left in the state because almost all wolves had been eradicated by hunting and trapping. In 1943, the first doe/fawn season was established. In 1954, two-thirds of the bucks that were killed during the gun season were less than three years old which was due to the extreme winter weather the state had experienced during the early 1950s.

Bub Franklin knew all these facts by heart and

many more, but that was not on his mind today. Today, he thought, I must kill a deer. He had five children at home, four girls and one boy who needed meat on their plates to fill their growing bodies. For several years in a row he had shot at least one deer, but last year had been an aberration that he did not want repeated. After two particularly harsh winters, the deer population in the state had been decimated. He had not even seen a deer within shooting range the previous season, so it was imperative that he not go two full seasons without filling his deer tag.

At age 18, he had joined the army and served two years of service leading up to World War II. He had been issued a Mauser Model 98 bolt action rifle. This was the same rifle that had been used in World War I. After basic training he waited nervously for deployment somewhere in the theater of war. He had been assigned a work detail to dislodge some boulders with a group of other enlistees when a rock dislodged and crashed onto his knee. The injury was severe, and he would walk with a limp the rest of his life. Because of the disability, he was given an honorable discharge along with a small disability pension for his service from the U.S. Army. He would have gladly given the pension back if the knee could be repaired, but the damage was significant and permanent. His one other compensation when he left the army was the Mauser Model 98 which the U. S. Army allowed him to keep when he was officially discharged.

He had the Mauser with him every year, thereafter. It was his "go to" gun for deer hunting and he found no reason to change to another model. It was a bolt action rifle with blade sights that was rugged and dependable. It had proven its worth in World War I and would shoot straight in any weather condition. The Mauser had served the army well in two world wars. Bub figured if the rifle was good enough for the army, it was good enough for him.

The Mauser was propped against a tree as he rested and let the air cool his heated brow. He was careful with the gun, cleaning it no matter how tired he was from the daily hunt. The blade sights were better than a scope for the type of shooting he would be doing. He hunted in high bluffs so most of his shooting would be into dense foliage. Likely, he would only get one shot, so he had to make sure that one shot counted.

These were his thoughts as he adjusted his hat, picked up his rifle, and started his slow limping gate towards a copse of trees that looked like a location where a deer might cross. After carefully looking over the terrain he settled in a spot where he had a good view in both directions. He had been sitting only a few minutes before he saw two gray squirrels scamper down an oak tree and commence a game of tag, chasing each other up and down several trees blissfully unaware that a hunter was only a few steps away. He continued to sit for another 45 minutes when a red fox sauntered by, caught a whiff of his scent, turned, and scurried off into the underbrush.

The buck arrived before he felt its presence; before he spotted it. One moment all was quiet, with nothing moving. The next moment the deer appeared, an apparition, a ghost from the wilderness. The first thing Bub saw was the massive horns. He stared at the horns a long moment before he noticed the body of the deer. The deer, unaware he was being watched by the hunter, would take a few steps, raise his head to look around, nose up, testing the air molecules for danger. The buck wasn't in a hurry. The deer came toward the opening slowly. He would take a step and look up, stop, look around, then another step, turning his head from side to side. His head remained up, nostrils flared, continuously testing the air for any sent that might represent danger.

Bub knew the deer was big, perhaps huge, but because of the undergrowth he could never get a full-on view of the animal. The buck kept moving slowly through a small clump of saplings. Bub did not feel the need to see the full body of the deer. He had seen enough to know it was a trophy deer once he saw the sun glinting off the antlers. Bub had shot plenty of large bucks in the past. This buck would join the list of other fine trophy bucks alongside the antlers that were tacked up on the rafters inside his garage.

What Bub was most interested in now, was the spot where he would kill the buck. He had to be patient and wait for the best location to take his one carefully aimed shot. If he missed with his first shot, the buck would be off, jumping, crashing through undergrowth, gone in a New York minute. He had done this before, finding just the right shooting lane using silence and patience to his advantage. Silent and patience were always the key to success when hunting deer. Bub's eyes looked and his mind calculated, until he saw the exact spot where he would kill the deer. The buck would have to cross one narrow spot where the undergrowth was stunted. He would be fully visible for only a few yards, feet really. This was the spot, the right spot; the ONLY spot to take the killing shot.

Even after all these years he still fought to calm his beating heart. Slow the breathing, he thought to himself, slow the breathing.

One shot. You only get one shot.

MAKE IT COUNT.

The Buck edged out into the opening. This was the first time Bub saw the height and width of the massive antlers. He didn't bother to count the number of points on the horns. There would be time for that after the kill. Massive, he thought, just a massive rack. Those were the only words that came to mind.

The Mauser came up to his shoulder, a movement so natural that he didn't have to think about the synapses that were already firing. One fluid motion and the gun was on his shoulder, his face kissing the stock of the gun like a long-departed lover. He looked down the metal sites, aligned the single front site and placed it in the groove of the back site.

'Two more steps, just take two more steps and you are dead.'

The buck, unaware of the hunter's presence, took those two tentative steps.

The gun exploded. Two birds flew from their perch in the tree above his head, the only witnesses to the shot. The buck jumped in the air and in one quick motion exploded back into the cover of forest, the only sanctity he knew. He crashed through berry briers and dead branches, catapulting small rocks, and kicked up dirt in his wake. The buck was off, leaping, hooves clattering in a race for his very existence.

For a moment, Bub stood paralyzed. He couldn't believe he had not delivered a killing shot. Had he hit a small branch he hadn't seen throwing the bullet off fractionally? Had the sites been knocked off kilter? Had he pulled the trigger a bit too hard instead of a gentle squeeze? He was perplexed. He had missed the kill shot. All he knew for sure is that he had no one to blame but himself.

As soon as he saw the buck jump in the air, he knew two things for sure. He knew the bullet had marked the buck, and he also knew the bullet had missed a vital organ.

He listened for the deer to crash, sweet forest music to a hunters' ear. That would have told him the buck was down, but there was no music, no crash.

Shit.   Goddamn.   Sonofabitch.

GODDAMNITALLTOHELL.

Those were his words, but they encompassed the words of every hunter who has ever shot and missed a deer in the killing zone.

After all these years his hands still shook.

What to do?

What to do?

What to do, NOW?

FIRST...... look for blood.

Yes, there was blood. Not a lot of blood but tracking blood just the same. It was almost noon. He could leave the deer and come back tomorrow, track the deer, and find it dead, for surely, it would die. He could find the deer tomorrow. Rigor mortis would have stiffened the muscles in death, the neck outstretched in one last gasp of oxygen. In a vain attempt to get up, the deer would make one last effort to run, run and hide.

Perhaps it was self-punishment for missing the kill shot, perhaps stubbornness, but for whatever reason he could not wait 'til tomorrow, wouldn't wait until tomorrow. He would wait a short time, but not for morning light. He would give it an hour, then track and kill the deer.

He waited. He made himself wait, something he was loath to do. He hated waiting. The seconds seemed like minutes, minutes like hours, the hour seemed like an eternity. When the hour was up, he set off in an awkward gate, one leg cooperating, the lame leg defiant.

He found the blood trail; he lost the blood trail. Must have hit it back from the lungs, he thought, probably low in the gut. He followed the thinning blood, kept looking for bits of lung but he knew there would not be any. Once he lost the trail altogether. He felt despondent until he found the trail again fifteen minutes later. On he went, listening, inspecting dried leaves that carpeted the forest floor, turning them over and looking for one leaf that might contain a few specks of blood.

He heard a shot in the distance, then another, then another still. His spirits sank a bit. It was in the direction of the blood trail. He trudged on, slowly. The knee was balky. He heard the rapid fire of more shots. Were there five or six shots in a row? The shots were closer now, rat, tat, tat, tat, tat, tat.

Why all the shooting? The hunter, whoever it was, wasn't moving because the shots seemed to all becoming from one stationary spot. Six more shots rang out, and then silence.

The last shots were close now, no more than a quarter of a mile away. Bub pushed on, gimpy leg and all. His shirt was soaked with perspiration. He wanted a drink but wouldn't allow the time to take his water out of his rucksack. He needed to know how this would end. He would take a step and swing the bad leg in front, then repeat the process. One smaller knoll to climb and he would be there.

Keep going . . . keep going . . . keep going.

Bub saw the hunter before he ever saw the buck. It was hard to miss the hunter because of his sheer size. The man sat on the ground his hunting jacket open at the waist. His eyes were glazed, and he was sweating profusely. The weight of the hunter had to be over 300 pounds. His gun, what was left of it, lay in pieces scattered around a small section of the ground. From what Bub could tell from the pieces of the rifle scattered about, was that the hunter had been firing a new Marlin Model 336 lever action rifle until his clip was empty. Bub could not be sure of the make and model of the rifle because there was not much of a gun left to identify. The stock was broken in two different places and the barrel was badly bent. Empty shell casings littered the ground.

When Bub located the body of the buck, he mentally began to picture what must have happened. He had certainly heard of inexperienced hunters getting buck fever, but this guy took the meaning of buck fever to an entirely differently level. The buck was mortally wounded but had managed to make it a mile from where Bub had shot it. Apparently, the hunter was so shocked by the sheer size of the deer that he freaked out and began firing indiscriminately. He would empty his gun, reload, and fire again.

The buck, exhausted, had fallen in a small ravine and could not get up. The man had then used the butt of his rifle to kill the deer and claim his prize. The beautiful antlers had been broken off by repeated blows which helped explain the condition of the gun. The head of the buck had been smashed, brain matter covered the bucks muzzle and one eye had popped out of the head and dangled outside the eye socket, a pulpy mess.

The fat man, still with a glazed look about him, finally began to realize what was happening. Words came gasping from his mouth.

"Mister get the hell away from my deer. I killed that deer fair and square and if you don't get away from my animal, I'll shoot you."

"Hell," said Bub, "You ain't shooting nobody. You ain't even got a gun left to shoot with. You smashed it all to hell on that beautiful deer."

Bub picked up his own rifle, took one last disgusted look at what had been a beautiful creature and started to walk away.

"Mister aren't you going to even help me dress this deer out?"

"He is your deer, buddy. It's your job to dress him out and get him out of here before he starts to rot. The weather is turning hot, so you better get to it."

Bud looked at his pocket watch. It was 2:30 in the afternoon and he had a two hour walk back to his car. He took a stride with his good leg and then swung the other leg in a shorter arc in front of him.

He would be back tomorrow with the early morning light. He still had to find and kill his own deer.

He would shoot a deer before the end of the season.

He had to.

His family was depending on him.

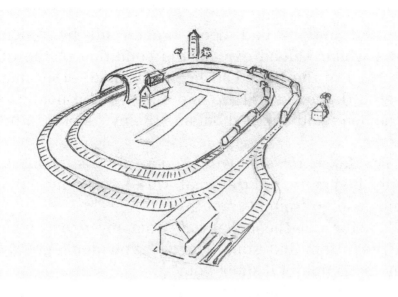

SKY HIGH
AND THE OLD POT LICKER

Do not tell me there isn't a crazy relative in your family, because that is just not possible. Every family has at least one relative where the bubble on the level does not quite line up in the center. Sometimes the bubble is a little to the left and other times it might be a bit to the right, but it is NEVER exactly between those two little dividing lines that indicate you are completely balanced.

You might mention to friends that the relative is a few cards short of a deck, or make a comment that the elevator doesn't go all the way to the top? Maybe they are the relative whose Intelligence Quotient doesn't exactly float the boat. They might be the relative who can't seem to hold down a job for any length of time because of their weirdness. Society often ostracizes people like that, and they are often seen as being too eccentric.

My family was lucky because we had two such relatives. We were fortunate because neither one of our relatives was a hurtful person. They simply couldn't differentiate between what was socially acceptable and what wasn't. Both relatives supplied us with endless amounts of entertainment in a tiny town where entertainment was often a rare commodity.

One of our cousin's given name was Floyd, although no one ever called him that. Many in our small river town wouldn't even know that Floyd was his given name. Everyone who knew him called him Lee High, or Sky-High Lee High.

His formal education ended at eighth grade and from there he entered the University of Hard Knocks. Education wasn't for him, at least not the kind of education that came from books.

He was out on his on his own by the time he was fifteen because he found it impossible to get along with his biological father. After dropping out of school, he started doing any odd jobs he could find. When it came to employment, he didn't care what the work entailed or what it paid. That was one of his good qualities because most of the jobs he took paid a paltry salary that barely kept him clothed and fed.

He seldom lasted on a job for more than a few weeks. If he managed to stay on a job for a month it was an exception. That is not to say that he lacked intelligence. He taught himself to operate all kinds of different machinery. He learned to operate a caterpillar and he could load and drive a dump truck. He could operate a bulldozer, an excavator and a backhoe. If it were mechanical, he would soon learn the intricacies of how to operate it.

If you gave him a sheet of paper and a pencil he would set down and sketch cartoon characters that were almost as good as artists who did it for a living. Unfortunately, sketching cartoon characters in a small town did not pay the bills, so he spent his time learning new skills. He was proficient in mixing and laying cement which landed him several odd jobs. He could make foundations for sidewalks and steps and mix the cement to finish the work. He was paid a pittance of what he would have made working for a unionized construction company. That never really seemed to bother him a great deal. If he had enough money in his pocket to buy a few meals at the local restaurant, he was satisfied.

When he was down on his luck, which occurred often, he would finagle a job as a bartender. He learned how to make every hard drink someone might order from memory. If he saw a drink made once or twice, he could commit it to memory. He would tend bar for a few weeks and dress up in a white shirt, but before long he would wear out his welcome. He might get in an argument with one of the customers and the bar owner would have no choice but to fire him; once again he would find himself out on the street looking for work.

He was offered a job in Vietnam operating a bulldozer for some foreign company that would have paid him an excellent wage and benefits. Who knows how he ever even heard about that job? "It's too damn far away and it's too damn hot over there," he would say. "Who the hell wants to go and work with all those spooks." Politically acceptable language was not one of his gifts. He turned the job down, of course.

Lee High would not have been able to find Vietnam on a map if his life depended on it. The truth was that he did not want to get far away from our small town on the Mississippi River. If he stayed close to the river, he knew he would be able to trap each fall and winter. Trapping was his default setting. Trapping allowed him to earn enough money to make it until springtime when he would be able to find another job. He was always better when he worked by himself, because there was no one else to argue with.

Two of my older brothers had gotten jobs working at an auto plant in Illinois building cars for Chrysler Corporation. They talked Lee High into coming along and applying for a job at the same plant. They knew he was down on his luck and could really use an infusion of cash. The money was good, and they found a small apartment where the rent was reasonable. Life was good and they got to work some overtime hours. What could possibly go wrong?

They worked at the Belvedere plant for a month before coming home for the first time. My brothers packed up their dirty clothes to take home for washing. Just as they were about to leave for the drive back to Wisconsin, they noticed that Lee High had packed up all his meager belongings into several well-worn bags and thrown them in the trunk of the car. My brothers glanced at each other and knew beyond a shadow of a doubt that Lee High was not coming back to Illinois with them.

They dropped Lee High off in our small town and agreed to meet up again on Sunday afternoon to drive back to Illinois. Lee High, of course, never showed up on Sunday. There was no explanation from him, no knock on the door, no telephone call. He was just a no show.

"Dammit," one of my brothers said, "I knew damn well once he threw all his belongings into the trunk of the car, he wasn't coming back with us."

The next time my brothers saw Lee High was a few months later, after both my brothers had been laid off from the auto plant. Lee High welcomed them back to our tiny village with a smile on his face and, as usual, never bothered to mention why he quit the job in Illinois.

You could get disgusted with Lee High on a regular basis, but you could never stay mad at him for long. He rolled with the punches and asked few favors. His car, when running, was an eyesore. In winter he would come to our house on the most bitter winter days to ask us to push his car to try and get it to start. Once the car was started, he would never stop to talk. He would roll down his window and give a short wave as he drove down the street, heading for the local restaurant for a cup of hot coffee. He didn't dare shut off the engine, so he would leave the car running until he was done with breakfast, which, depending on who he was talking to, could be an hour or more. He never put more than a dollar's worth of gas in his car and it was not uncommon for the car to run out of gas while Lee High was eating breakfast.

Lee High did have one unique talent. He was great at getting people to spend more money than they planned on. Whenever there was a town event, Lee High would be there selling tip ups. He would tie on a money belt and circulate around the crowd.

"Oh, by god, you can afford to buy more than five dollars-worth of tip ups," he'd say, "it's for a damn good cause." Sure enough, people would take out their wallets and fork over a little more money than they had planned on. He never had any money himself, but he was particularly good at getting people who had money to spend, spend, spend. He played on the local adult baseball team although, honestly, he was a terrible player. He rode the bench every game, but when it came time to pass the hat, he would be the one who walked up into the stands, held out his grungy baseball cap and asked folks to contribute a few bucks for the betterment of the team. He single-handedly kept the baseball program afloat by getting spectators to contribute a little more money than they had anticipated.

Lee High was getting older and one of my brothers was trying to get him to accept Social Security payments that were rightfully his. Wouldn't you know that for some unknown reason, he adamantly refused to sign up for social security benefits. He could have really used the money, but he had it in for the government for some reason that none of us understood and he flat out refused to accept the small monthly payments from the government. In his mind, the government had somehow done him wrong and he wasn't about to accept their money. That just is the way Lee High was. You could not change him. He would get some idea in his head and then could not get it out.

He had a type of epilepsy, or palsy, that would cause his eyes to roll back in his head. When an episode occurred, he would swoon and black out for a short period of time. It was a scary thing to behold and it made us who sometimes witnessed these spells, incredibly nervous. We really didn't understand this medical condition. The episodes never lasted exceptionally long. After a few minutes he would wake up and act as if nothing had ever happened. It was one of these episodes that finally killed him. He had an episode while driving his old beater car down the road, had an accident, rolled his car and was med flighted to the nearest city. He died the same day.

He lived by Henry Ford's admonition: "Never complain, and never explain."

You might think his funeral would be small. After all, he had no money. When word of his passing spread through the town, it was all people could talk about. The whole town turned out for the visitation. Lee High, with all his faults was still one of our own. Yes, he was undependable and would spend every dime he ever made, but he was talented, funny, and creative. You loved him one minute, hated him the next, but he belonged to the fabric of the town. He knew everyone, and everyone knew him. He was a character, but he was the town's character, and when he died part of the town died with him. Every small town needs an eccentric soul and Lee High fit that bill to a T.

The other family character was our brother-in-law everyone called, "Beans." His real name was Bernard, but everyone in town called him "Beans." He was called "Beans" because almost everyone in town thought he was full of beans, so the nickname stuck. His entire career revolved around working for the railroad that passed near town. He was one of those guys who felt he never worked a day in his life. He loved everything about the railroad and would regale anyone who cared to listen, and many who didn't, about the history of the railroad.

The trouble was you couldn't believe a word he said. He could stretch the truth like no one else. You could never be sure where the truth ended, and the falsehoods began.

Once he retired, he set up a large model train track that covered the entirety of his basement. He would get up each morning and start up the train and let it run continuously throughout the day. Trains and train stories were his main hobby. He liked to fish and he hunted deer each fall. He only shot one deer in all the years he hunted. He wouldn't stand for more than an hour when hunting and then would start wandering around scaring any deer in the area. The one small doe he finally shot was curled up sleeping. He walked up on the deer while hunting on one of the islands of the Mississippi River. It still took him three shots to subdue the one-hundred-pound yearling.

He liked to fish, but never owned a boat of his own. He was dependent on us to take him fishing on warm summer days. He would bait up with a worm, cast out on the backwater of the Mississippi River and wait for a bite. He preferred to fish for sunfish although he would occasionally catch some other type of fish. None of us would catch every fish that we hooked, and Beans was certainly no exception to that rule. If he lost a fish, he would always say the same thing, "That pot licker was a bass. By god that was a big fish." If we heard that exclamation once, we heard it a thousand times. Every fish that got off was always a 'pot licking bass.' He used that expression every time we ever went fishing. If he would have caught every bass, he said he had on, he would have swamped the boat.

"Beans," the "Old Pot Licker," has passed into family lore just like "Sky High Lee High." They were characters to be sure, but they made our life more interesting. We laughed at their stories, and often at their antics. We sometimes laughed at them, but more often laughed with them. We never knew for sure if their stories and antics were true, but they always entertained us with their actions, deeds, and words. Sometimes you would believe the stories they told, but many times you didn't.

If you have ever lived in a small town where everybody knows everybody, then you have known the "Sky Highs" and the "Pot Lickers" of this world and you are usually better off for it.

OLD BONES

Little Flower turned to her husband, Black Bear, and said, "The white soldiers lie again. They never tell the truth. I was a young girl when the white military told us we could live here in peace and raise our corn by the river. Our chiefs signed a treaty, but now I am an adult, a mother with a child, and the whites have broken the treaty many times. The white men have been coming on our land for as many years as I have lived. They trample our corn fields leaving us with little left to eat. They dig holes in the ground and take out the rocks that have value, but they give us nothing in return for being on our land."

"Now they want us to move again. This time they tell us to move to the other side of the big river. They have promised us enough corn to make it through the winter if we agree to move. We are Sauk warriors and are willing to die to defend our land, but many of our people do not want to move from our ancestral home. Our Chief, the one the white men call Keokuk, wants the braves to fight, but Makataimeshekiakiak (Ma-ka-tai-me-she-kia-kiak), called Black Hawk, says it would be foolish to fight the white soldiers. Our two chiefs do not get along. This is our home, our land, where we have always lived. Now we, the white soldiers say, must move again. What good is the treaty with the white men if they always break it?"

"You are right, Little Flower, but we cannot fight the white soldiers. They have too much power and too many weapons. We are Sauk farmers who turn over the earth to raise our crops. Now they promise to give us enough corn so we can survive the winter and plant our gardens with the coming spring rains. The braves do not like this. Many of our braves want to fight, but we have no chance against the power of the white soldiers."

ONE YEAR LATER

"We will be going back now, Little Flower. Our son, Prairie Dog, is eight full seasons old. He is old enough to help us with the planting and harvesting of the corn. The white army did not give us enough corn to survive the winter and many of our people have died, especially the young and the old. Once again, the white soldiers have spoken false words. Black Hawk has gathered four hundred warriors and twelve hundred women, children and old men. Our people are hungry and angry. Our warriors want to fight, and Black Hawk thinks the Ho Chunk Nation will join our cause and fight alongside us if we go to war with the white soldiers. The British may also join forces and fight with us as well. They do not like the white soldiers and would like to see them defeated. We will go back to our homeland now. We must resist the whites who continue to come onto the land that was promised to us in the treaty we were forced to sign. We do not want war. We want to live in peace and go back to our homes on the other side of the river and plant our corn fields. The white settlers have come more and more onto our land and we must be prepared to fight if necessary or we will have no home to return to. Gather your things and be ready to leave in the morning. Watch after Prairie Dog. He is not a strong boy. He has weakness from lack of food just like many of our young. I know you worry about him each day."

In the morning, the Sauk Indians had gathered up their belongings and traveled back across the great river to start their return trip home. Even with their ever-present hunger pangs, everyone was in a joyful mood, thinking of their ancestral home. Suddenly the Indians heard shouting, and gunfire erupted. Members of the Illinois Militia had been called out and were firing on men, women and children without warning. The Sauk Indians were ill prepared for battle as they only possessed hatchets and knives. The battle raged on for over an hour with each side taking casualties.

Little Flower, Prairie Dog, and Black Bear were temporarily separated during the battle, but they regrouped after the skirmish ended. The Sauk Indians regrouped and some of the warriors heard that Black Hawk had sent a messenger to negotiate a peace settlement, but rather than meet with the messenger, the white soldiers killed him.

Black Bear tells Little Flower, "Now we have no choice, we have to fight for the lives of our people. Some of our braves have already found smaller settlements of whites and are killing and scalping them. We must leave here with as many of our tribe that are able to ride or walk. We must cross back over the big river and make our way north. If we are lucky and do not meet more soldiers along the way, we will be able to make it to Canada where we will start a new life. It will be an exceedingly difficult journey and there will be many setbacks. Many of our people will die before we reach Canada, but we have no choice, we cannot return to our native land."

"Little Flower, we have to try and save our son."

"We have no food," said Little Flower. "There aren't that many horses. Most of us will have to walk. I know if we stay here, we will die. I will go with you, but I fear for our son. Let us talk of this no more and hope that Ma-Ka-Tai-Me-She-Kia-Kiak will lead us north and save us from the white soldiers."

They stayed to the wooded areas as much as possible, crossed over the big river and camped deep in the forest. Fires were kept at a minimum and scouts were posted at night, always on the lookout for soldiers.

The white soldiers followed the Indians when possible and there were skirmishes as they traveled north. The army sent out troops and militia from various towns who had joined forces to fight the Indians. Many of the Sauk braves died at the hands of the soldiers who were well-armed. Sometimes the skirmishes involved several hundred combatants, while other times it might be as few as a dozen.

The Indians had now been traveling for three weeks with little water and practically no food. They had no choice but to start butchering some of their horses so they would have something to eat. Hunger gnawed at them each day, a constant companion. They buried their dead at night. They were always on the lookout for the soldiers. Little Flower woke one morning with her tongue swollen to twice its normal size. She had consumed no water for the past three days.

"I cannot talk," she mumbled to her husband. "My tongue is too big. Prairie Dog will not wake up. He has had no food for three days. If we cannot find food and water soon, he will die."

Later that day they traveled past two large lakes. There they found fresh water to drink and Black Bear used a sharpened stick to spear two fish near the shore. He roasted the fish over an open fire and fed most of the fish to Prairie Dog and Little Flower.

They camped near the lakes for two days before traveling on. They broke camp and walked on for several more days before encountering militia near a settlement on the banks of a small stream. Fighting raged on and off for most of the day with 80 fighting Sauk warriors killed or wounded. With each passing day the terrain began to change, the bluffs became higher and more difficult to climb, especially for the women, children, and old people. They had been on the move for more than two full moons and everyone was exhausted. They had to kill one more horse to keep from starving.

In the morning they traveled with the sun, always heading west. They had not seen the big river for many days, but they knew it was to the west of where they were, so they traveled on, always on the lookout for militia. If they could make it to the big river and somehow cross it, they might be able to reach safety. Perhaps the soldiers would not chase them further and return to their own homes. Saukenuk, their home village was no longer in their thoughts. Their corn fields would not be planted this year even though it was past the season for putting seeds in the ground. No corn would spring from the earth in tiny green chutes. The women would not be watering and hoeing in attempts to make the corn grow tall. All the fleeing Sauk band could do now was to rise with the sun and travel north and west.

They buried the dead when they found them, always at night. No one spoke of the dead. There were no more tears to be shed, emotions had died with the fallen. They avoided any settlements and kept to the woods and gullies that offered the most safety. They would eat anything they could find, pulling the bark from dead trees looking for ants and grubs. When they found a stream, they would camp nearby and look for frogs, crayfish, or minnows.

That night they all went to sleep with empty stomachs. Little Flower awoke during the night and left her husband's side when she heard Prairie Dog coughing. His head was extremely hot to the touch. All she had to give him was water.

Black Bear and Little Flower slept on the ground the rest of the night with Prairie Dog between them. His breathing was shallow, his face flushed, and his body looked like the scarecrows they put in their corn fields to scare away birds. They had to find more food before they all died.

They were seeing more signs of settlers. Most were farmers with plowed fields, split rail fences, and wooden houses. Black Bear, Little Flower, and Prairie Dog had to wait in the deep shadows of the woods with the rest of the band until the sun went down before they felt safe moving away from the settlers.

When the sun came up the next morning, they followed it as it moved west, toward their destiny with the big river. They would have to find a shallow place to cross the river and then turn north toward Canada. That was where their destiny lay.

They had been traveling for most of the summer and watched as their numbers dwindled. The old died first, followed by the young. Every few days another grave had to be dug. They were passing limestone bluffs dotted with hardwood forests. They made camp that night too exhausted to chase the mosquitoes that buzzed around them and sucked their blood.

The next morning Black Bear was up early looking for something his wife and son could eat. Little Flower found him as the sun was ascending over the high bluffs. As soon as Black Bear spotted Little Flower, he saw the indescribable sorrow on her face. She told her husband that Prairie Dog had died during the night. Black Bear picked up his son, light as a feather, skin stretched over protruding bones. They buried their son on the crest of a hill where his spirit could look out over the valley below.

After the burial of Prairie Dog, Little Flower refused to go on. She wanted to lie with her son and go with him to the afterlife. Black Bear told her they would have another son when they were safe in Canada. She did not believe him, but he was her husband, a man she had always obeyed. As the other tribe members started walking on, she took a last long look at the crest of the hill where her son was buried. She moved on with the others, but her spirit was dead.

Two days later they glimpsed the big river through the canopy of oak, walnut and maple trees. They headed north, keeping the river in sight, looking for a shallow crossing spot on the wide river.

On the fourth day they finally came to a spot where the river was wide and shallow. Stumps stuck out above the waterline. They lashed logs together with vines to make crude rafts. The rafts would make the crossing easier for the women, old men, and children. They had finally found a place where they thought it safe to attempt a river crossing. They cut long poles to push them across the river to Iowa and safety.

The next morning, they began loading the rafts with the young and the elderly. Fighting broke out almost immediately. There was gunfire from the shore and a large boat appeared in the river. The large guns began shooting indiscriminately at the children and the old with no regard to taking prisoners. Bodies fell into the water and others jumped in the river attempting to avoid the guns. The water ran red with their blood.

Black Bear was running with Little Flower across a hilltop when shooting erupted. The shooting was from military forces and Indian bands siding with the militia forces. Little Flower witnessed Black Bear when he was shot. The bullet hit him in the side, and he rolled down an incline. Little Flower found him hidden behind bushes and somehow got him to his feet. She half carried and half dragged him to the edge of a bluff. She noticed a rock formation and pulled Black Bear towards it. Bushes around the rocks hid a small opening. Little Flower pushed Black Bear into the small opening and squeezed in behind him. She clasped her hand over the wound, but blood oozed out between her fingers.

She lay down beside Black Bear and kept her hand

clamped over the wound. The fighting was still intense, but no one found the opening where they were hidden. They stayed where they were, hidden from view until the sun started to set. For the first time since Black Bear had been shot, he spoke to Little Flower.

"You must wait until it is dark and then make it to the river. If you find a raft you will be able to cross the river at night. You can still make it to Canada. There will be Sauk and Fox Indians hidden near the river and they will help you."

Little Flower looked at her husband before she spoke. "My spirit died with Prairie Dog. I would have gladly died then with Prairie Dog and joined his spirit in the other world. I will go no farther. I do not want to live in a world with white people that have lied and cheated, taken our land and killed our people. When I arrive in the afterlife, I hope there are no white men living there."

With her speech finished she lay down beside Black Bear and held him close. Black Bear died sometime during the night. She stayed with the body of her husband for three more nights. She refused to eat or drink until the great spirit took her to the afterlife.

1957

Jim and John Boylan had tried to buy the farm from Spencer Sutherland several times before. They had offered what they thought was an honest price, but Spencer refused every offer. He was known locally as the tightest man in the county. If someone asked the price for a cow, or a bale of hay, the price was always too low for Sutherland. The farm had been in the

Sutherland family for 150 years and if he had his way it would remain in the family for another 150 years.

That opinion changed one day when he got up from his chair, clutched his heart, and fell to his kitchen floor while drinking his third cup of morning coffee. A farm worker found him where he fell, and Spencer was rushed to the nearest hospital where he spent the next month recovering. A near death experience can change any man, even a man like Spencer Sutherland. As he lay in the hospital bed recovering from his heart attack, it dawned on him that farming might not be in his future. When he got out of the hospital, he called Jim Boylan and offered, for the first time in his life, a fair price for his farm.

The Boylan brothers couldn't get out their check books fast enough. No man not named Sutherland, had ever set foot on the farm that overlooked the Mississippi River valley. The legal papers were signed within two weeks and Spencer Sutherland bought a camper trailer that same afternoon and promptly took off for Florida before the ink had dried on the sales contract.

Jim and John Boylan were avid hunters. They couldn't wait a second longer to walk their new property and look for deer sign. They drove out to the land, parked their truck, and took their first steps on land they never thought they would own. They were giddy with excitement. The first thing they did was look at the breathtaking views from the edge of the bluffs that overlooked the Mississippi River. They had been walking for two hours, taking their time, pleased with the deer sign they were seeing, making plans for the fall hunt. They looked for locations where they might build deer stands. They were at the crest of a bluff that overlooked the islands that dotted the Mississippi River.

It was while looking at the islands that Jim first noticed the large rock outcropping that was partially hidden by the trees that grew around the rocks. They decided to look at the rock formation and climbed down to get a closer view. This wasn't level farmland, something the Sutherlands only seemed interested in, so it was quite possible no one else had been to this spot in ages. They were just about to climb back up to the crest of the hill when John Boylan noticed a crack in the rock formation. John got down on his hands and knees, cleared away some debris, and crawled into a small space that was not quite tall enough to stand up in. He called out to his brother, who soon joined him.

The first thing that John noticed, once he got used to the dim light, were the bones. He called to his brother to crawl in to join him. They looked down on the remains of human bones. Some of the bones had been scattered about by animals, but the skulls were intact, and the vertebrae were easily identifiable. The sinew and cartilage had ossified and there were small teeth marks on some of the bones where animals had gnawed on them. Once they knew what they were looking at they quickly crawled out of the rocks, marked the location with a red bandanna and quickly drove home to call the police.

The police took a few days to respond. Apparently old bones didn't take the same priority as traffic accidents, or perhaps the police thought the Boylan brothers didn't know the difference between human bones and the bones of a wild animal. When the forensic team finally arrived and crawled inside the rock outcropping, they quickly recognized that the bones were in fact, human.

The police carefully loaded the bones into a cardboard box and told the Boylan brothers they would be sending the bones to the state crime lab in Madison.

The next day the bones were sealed in another box and transported to the state crime lab via state vehicle. Since the bones were obviously human, they became a priority assignment. They were photographed from different angles, and samples of the bones were put under microscopes. One of the bodies was identified as male and the other as female. The bones were certainly old, but their exact age was indeterminate due to age and degradation. Based on the size of the bones, it was determined that both were from mature adults.

The Boylans received a telephone call from the crime lab a few days later, but there wasn't much that was newsworthy. They were told the bones would remain in custody of the State Crime Lab, but nothing new had been uncovered as to who the deceased were, or what they had died from.

"Well, said Jim Boylan, what do you think of that phone call?"

"All I can say for sure," said his brother, "is that those bones have been in that crevice for a long, long time."

The same day two lab assistants at the State Crime Lab placed the bones in a sealed box, labeled it with an identification number and transported the bones to the lock up area. The box was placed on a metal shelf, the final resting place for the bones.

"It's too bad we don't have better technology," said one of the lab assistants. If we had better technology, we might find out who this man and woman were and how they died."

"Ya," said the other assistant, "there are new discoveries in forensic science every decade or so. Maybe someday we will know not just how this man and woman died, but also how they lived."

THE GOOD WARDEN

The two young brothers passed by a sign each day. They didn't like the sign but there was nothing they could do about it. They were just kids and the sign had been put up by the Department of Natural Resources. It read: Fish Restocking Program. No Public Fishing Allowed. Violators will be prosecuted to the full extent of the law. No Trespassing.

The sign was well weathered. The sign had been erected several years prior. During the Great Depression, the federal government created public works projects in an attempt to reignite the failed U.S. economy and crawl out of the Depression. The U. S. government employed local labor, predominantly from impoverished rural towns and villages to do manual labor. In towns across America, money was appropriated by the federal government for the purpose of creating work for thousands of men who were unemployed. In this small river town where just about everyone was unemployed, money was finally being appropriated for the purpose of creating four ponds of approximately equal size and shape. Once the ponds were completed, the local laborer force was done with the project. The ponds were designed for raising fish. The largest pond was approximately a half mile long and several hundred yards wide. The smallest pond was little more than a good-sized pothole. Cement drainage canals were built between each pond allowing water to flow in either direction. There were wooden, screened panels that could be raised or lowered between each pond.

The public works projects allowed local laborers to earn enough in wages to be able to feed and clothe their families as they limped through the worst downturn in the economy that anyone had ever experienced. It was only later that the term was coined, "The Great Depression."

It was through the depression years that government assistance programs provided work and helped save many families from going without the basics of food and shelter. The wages were often a dollar a day, barely enough to put food on the table; but men flocked to sign up for a chance to work and earn some much-needed money to support their families.

The project of creating the ponds took several years. When the project was nearly finished the Department of Natural Resources built a house along the bank of the largest pond. The house, once completed, would be the residence of a game warden whose job it was to look after the ponds and supervise the stocking of fish that would be transplanted into the ponds. The warden was to marshal the Upper Mississippi River Waterway. He had the legal jurisdiction to issue citations for anyone breaking the law. The house that the warden was to occupy during his tenure was christened the "State House" by locals because it was built with state resources.

The game warden was a busy man. He had a great deal of land and water to cover to enforce the law. The Depression often caused law- abiding citizens to be more concerned about their families' empty bellies than following laws set forth by the federal government. Not everyone got a job in the Public Works Projects. There were always more applicants than jobs. Those men who didn't land a government sponsored job had to find other ways to feed their families.

It was hard for parents to watch their children going to bed with empty stomachs. Squirrels, rabbits, game birds, deer, even muskrats made their way to the frying pan and cooking pots of many families. Food was scarce and anything that was edible found a place at the dinner table.

The wardens had to uphold the law and hold those responsible who broke the law. Those who broke laws were given a citation and required to pay a fine for their transgressions. if they didn't have the money to pay the fine, they could be jailed, but then the government would have to feed them. Some wardens went strictly by the letter of the law while others took a more introspective view of what they allowed to go on during their tenure. Some wardens didn't exactly look the other way when laws were broken, but sometimes they had selective hearing and eyesight. After all the wardens had families of their own to feed and clothe and they were quite cognizant the country was in the throes of a deep depression. The more lenient wardens might not go out of their way to "pinch" someone who shot a deer out of season if they knew the family had numerous mouths to feed.

If a man shot a deer out of season and tried to sell the venison and was later caught in the act of doing so, wardens would arrest him. It was The Depression and there were often two sets of rules that applied, or not applied, to those who technically broke the law.

The warden had to consider the circumstances surrounding the law that had been broken. Was it a major offense where the warden had no choice but to arrest the offending party, or might he look the other way if he deemed it a minor violation? The personality of the game warden often defined whether a man was arrested or just given a warning. Sometimes the warden looked past the law if he knew that throwing a man in jail would put his family in dire straits without money or food to put on the table. Simply put, during The Depression the definition of the law was up to interpretation and the conscience of the warden.

The current warden was a strict interpreter of the law. He was unmarried and had been living in the State House for nearly three years. He was not a popular figure in the village because he thought any violator should be written up. He cited all lawbreakers and slept well at night doing so.

He even went so far as to question the two young boys who looked longingly at the ponds each day.

"What are you kids doing down here? I see you every day looking at these ponds. You know you can't fish in these waters. These are stock ponds for raising fish. No one can fish here. If I catch you fishing, I'm going to have to cite you for breaking the law."

"You get on home now before you get in trouble. I'm going to keep an eye on you two and I better not ever catch you fishing in these ponds."

The boys, of course never said a word to the warden. They really wanted to fish because they knew the ponds were well stocked with both pan fish and game fish. They watched pan fish rising each day greedily sucking in mayflies that lay on the ponds surface. They also knew that they couldn't get in trouble with the warden, so they turned around, bowed their heads, and headed home.

Two weeks later they noticed a strange car at the State House. A man was taking things from the car and carrying them into the house. They stayed back a good distance, not wanting to get into trouble with the warden. After a few more trips into the house the man noticed the boys and beckoned them over.

"Hello," he said, "I saw you standing over there and I could use some help unpacking my car. I'm Doug Folger, the new game warden. Would you care to give me a hand carrying my gear in the house?"

The boys were nervous, but they slowly nodded in agreement. Doug loaded them up with bundles of clothes, pots and pans, dishes and silverware, and showed them where to put everything once they got inside the house. When they were done, Doug offered each of the boys a dime.

"No, Sir" said the boys, "Our parents wouldn't allow us to take any money. Besides, we had a good time helping you get settled in."

"Well, you come back anytime," said Doug. "I owe you a favor."

A week later the boys were again walking past the ponds when a car drove up behind them. When they saw it was the new warden, they were sure they were in trouble. They hung their heads and hoped they weren't going to embarrass their parents and get into trouble.

"Hey, boys, I see you are headed for the ponds."

The boys put their heads down and started to apologize. "No, no," said Doug, "you have nothing to apologize for."

"Why, did you think you were doing something wrong?"

The boys were now really nervous, but they managed to stammer out, "We are really sorry. The warden that was here before you warned us to stay away from the ponds because they were used for raising fish. We know the sign says, No Fishing, Violators Will Be Prosecuted.

Doug looked at the boys before saying, "I can't even read that sign. It's so weather beaten I don't think anyone could read that sign."

"I'll tell you something boys, I've got a problem. There are way too many fish in these ponds. Pretty soon they will get stunted from overpopulation and start dying off from some parasitic disease. You boys could do me a real favor if you'd come down here and catch some of those fish. I'd really appreciate it. You'd be doing me a big favor. What do you say?"

The boys couldn't quite register what the warden was saying. All they had ever heard from the previous warden was that they couldn't fish in the ponds and now they were being told they should fish in the ponds.

They looked at the warden, then looked at each other and began grinning from ear to ear. The only thing they stammered out to the warden was, "Could we start fishing today?"

Now it was the wardens turn to smile. "No time like the present, so you better get on home and dig some worms."

They did just that. They dug a can of worms, grabbed their cane poles, and shot down the road to the third pond. They baited up and tossed their lines into the water about six feet from shore. In less than thirty seconds their corks went under and one of the boys pulled out a large sunfish. As that fish was landed his brother pulled out a huge crappie.

It only took them thirty minutes to catch as many fish as they needed for their family. They cut a notched willow and threaded it through the gills of the fish and used that as their stringer. They walked up the road with a stringer full of fat fish, some of which were dragging along the ground. They switched off carrying the fish until they got home.

Their parents couldn't believe the boys had received permission to fish in the ponds. They questioned them thoroughly about what the warden had said. Once the inquisition was over, the fish were cleaned, and their mother fried them with garden potatoes, and they ate the best supper they had eaten in a long time.

For the rest of the summer, up until it was time to go back to school, they fished each day if the weather permitted. The warden saw the boys at least once a week. The boys had the feeling the warden made it a point to check in with them. He would always comment what a fine mess of fish they had caught, and he made a point to say, "Keep doing what you're doing. There are still too dang many fish in those ponds. You have to help me decrease the population."

They caught sunfish and crappie, bullheads and catfish, bass and northern pike. They would watch large bass chase small skip jack shad into the shallows. When the bass got too close to the skip jacks and were just about to catch them, the skip jacks would head towards shore and launch themselves out of the water and up on the bank. When the bass passed by, the shad would flop around on the ground until they managed to flip back into the water and swim away to live another day.

The warden stayed in the small town for three years before he was transferred to his next posting. He had been happy living in the State House and was sorry to leave. He had seen the two boys grow and mature and enter high school. When it was time for the warden to leave for his next posting, a party was thrown in his honor. He was given a standing ovation because he was so much different from the previous warden, who, the townspeople said, "never gave anybody a break."

The two brothers showed up at the State House the day before the warden was scheduled to depart. They asked if they could help carry his things out to the car. He told the boys that one of his last acts as warden had been to petition the state to open all four ponds for public fishing. That was his parting gift to the small town that was just now starting to crawl out of the Depression.

The boys walked Doug out to his car the morning he was leaving. They hugged one another and tears trickled down their faces. As the warden was pulling out of his driveway, he rolled down his window and said, "Just because I'm leaving that doesn't give you the right to fall down on your job. Keep catching those fish. There are still too darn many fish in those ponds."

The ponds are still there today. There are fish in the ponds, not as many fish as there used to be, but they are still there. A few of the older residents still fish the ponds on warm summer days. If they are patient, they usually come home with enough fish for their supper.

THE GRADER MAN
AND TWO HUGE TROUT

Dean Everson worked for the county where he had spent his entire life. He drove a road grader 50 weeks out of the year filling in potholes and smoothing out bumps. When he wasn't moving gravel from one spot to another, he was mowing tall grass as it bent and encroached on the edge of the roads. The county Dean lived in was one of the most sparsely populated in the state. The population of the entire county was no more than 14,000 residents. The lack of residents with few employment opportunities combined to make it one of the poorest counties in the state. The county residents were poorly compensated by financial rewards, but they did take a great deal of pride in residing in one of the most beautiful counties in the state. The tax base of the county was representative of the residents who chose to live there. There wasn't much for tax revenue and there were no large businesses in the county where residents could work and make a decent living. Dean felt lucky when he landed a job working for the county, although his wages were just barely over the minimum.

Dave and his wife Dorothy raised a large family which was the norm, rather than the exception, for the rural county they lived in. Not many local folks seemed to know for an absolute certainty just how many Everson kids there were. When asked, locals might say, "They live so far out in the sticks who the hell knows how many youngins they got running around out there." When the subject came up, which it seldom did, people might venture guesses as to the definitive number of children they had sired. Locals speculated the number of Everson children was around eight, or ten, or possibly twelve children, depending on who was venturing the opinion. To locals it wasn't a subject that garnered a great deal of interest.

The family lived in a ramshackle house on a one lane gravel road, about ten miles outside of the nearest small town. People said the Everson's were farmers, but, they agreed, it was a mighty small operation. They raised a little tobacco as a cash crop, and they planted a few acres of corn and soybeans. They owned a small assortment of scrawny Holstein cows that required milking twice a day and planted a huge garden that supplied them with sweet corn, potatoes, radishes, onions, cucumbers, tomatoes, watermelons, cabbages and beets. What they didn't eat during the growing season got canned and put on the pantry shelves for the winter months.

They rarely came to town. They saw no need to fill gas in the car for a drive to town when they were self-sufficient on the farm. They minded their own business and were well liked by neighbors. Their children were well behaved. The clothes the children wore to school were clean, but well worn. In that sense, they were not a lot different from other families in the area. Their children were clothed, fed and loved, even if money was in short supply.

The issue of money was ongoing. Dean was quite content with his job driving a grader for the county even though his salary hardly covered the cost of keeping his family clothed and fed. He liked the fact that he could work alone. He would smooth out the gravel on the rural county roads and take out the washboard divots that would invariably pop up.

In the fall, he would hunt raccoon with a cur farm dog and sell the pelts to a local buyer. The coon pelts brought in a few more precious dollars that helped pay for presents nestled under the tree when Christmas rolled around.

His nearest neighbors knew he would occasionally harvest a deer out of season. They would hear a rifle late at night and figure there was one less deer roaming the woods. Local folks didn't like it if people poached deer out of season, but if there was a need to feed a large family an exception was made without much of a comment.

Dean worked on gravel roads five days a week with dust billowing up around him. Each morning his wife would pack a substantial lunch in his battered metal lunch pail knowing she would not see him again until she heard the grader pull into the driveway late in the afternoon. When he was in his grader and working, he was his own boss. He didn't have to work with anyone else and if his section of gravel roads were well maintained, no one was going to complain. Everyone who drove the gravel roads he maintained knew the quality of his work was excellent.

There was one section of road he particularly enjoyed. The road was a stone's throw away from a trout stream. This section of road split and branched off in two different directions. There was a grassy triangle where the road split that offered enough space for him to park his grader. There was shade from overhanging branches that offered him relief from the summer sun. It was a peaceful spot where he could hear the gurgling of the stream in the distance and enjoy his lunch in peace. He would work on this section of road once a week and he always took the opportunity to enjoy a leisurely lunch out of the direct sun.

One day he finished his lunch a little early and decided to stroll down by the stream. He knew this section of the stream well. There were no deep pools where trout could hold and languidly rise to sip hatching insects. There were few riffles where some trout could hide and have an easy food source drifting by in a foot of fast-moving water. The land by the edge of the stream wasn't high enough to provide an undercut bank where trout could wait unseen in shadows to ambush unsuspecting prey.

He walked gingerly along, unwinding the kinks in his back and neck. The sun was high overhead. He knew he would soon have to climb back onto the grader and finish his day's work. He was just about to turn around when he saw a flat section of water that was no more than a few feet deep. He didn't know what made him look at this particular spot of water because there wasn't anything special about it. Just as he was about to turn and leave, something suddenly caught his eye. He took a second look and couldn't believe what he was seeing. There were two exceptionally large fish lying side-by-side in water no more than three feet deep. Both fish were in a holding pattern moving their tails just enough to maintain their position.

Dean was by no means an expert fisherman nor was he an authority on trout. He was too busy trying to feed and clothe his family to take time out from his daily schedule to fish on a regular basis. At first glance he didn't know what kind of fish he was seeing, but after a closer inspection he saw spots on the sides of the fish. Some spots were red inside white circles while others were black spots inside white circles. Once he saw the telltale spots, he knew these fish had to be German brown trout. Not only were they brown trout, but they were also, he realized, the largest trout he had ever seen.

Dean had caught a few trout before on those rare occasions when he had time to fish, but he was no expert when it came to catching trout. He had caught small trout in deep pools using a cane pole, a bobber, and a worm for bait. He knew real trout fishermen would never use a cane pole. Trout this size would easily break the line on a cane pole and would certainly get away and he might never have another chance to catch them. If he wanted to land these two trout, he would have to fish with something better than a cane pole to accomplish it.

He kept looking at the trout when his shadow suddenly passed over the water. Both trout were off in a flash, propelled like rockets. He waited a few minutes and was ready to head back to his grader when he saw the two trout coming back down the stream pushing a wake of water in front of them. He crouched low so he wouldn't be seen. Both trout came back to their original location, turned, and resumed the same holding pattern they had been in before.

This must be their home pool, he thought, even though the water wasn't very deep. Dean stayed in a crouched position and backed out slowly so he wouldn't spook the trout again. His mind was churning as he walked back to his grader. His hands were shaking so badly it took him three tries to get the engine to turn over. He knew somehow, he had to catch these two trout, but he had no idea how he was going accomplish the task. You couldn't easily sneak up on them because they would spot you and be off in a flash. He decided he must think his strategy over carefully and come up with a plan.

Once he got home from work, he went directly to his barn. He had an old casting rod and an even older, beat up reel that had been gathering dust on one of the rafters. He tested the line and it seemed in decent shape. He tried to break the line with his hands and was happy to see he couldn't. Okay, so the line would hold. The reel didn't cast particularly well but he thought he could get it to cast at least twenty feet. He dug some worms and tied a good-sized hook on the line.

He was ready.

He hoped the trout were as well.

He was becoming obsessed with the idea of catching the two trout, so two days later found him back at the stream after he had finished his shift on the grader. He crouched as low as he could and saw that the two trout were still in the shallow pool of water. He baited his hook with a fat, wiggling worm and cast as far upstream as he could. His strategy was to let the current take the bait toward the trout. He waited a few minutes but there was no tug on the line. Curiosity got the better of him, so he raised himself up into a half crouch to get a peek at the trout. As soon as he rose, both trout took off like speeding bullets. He was so disgusted with himself he threw the pole down in frustration.

He had just finished reeling in his line when he saw the wake in the water. The trout were returning to their home pool, but he could tell by the rapid movement of their tails they were skittish and ready to bolt at any movement, so he slowly backed away and drove dejectedly back to the farm.

He stopped at the stream a few days later. He had gone out at night and caught some night crawlers and wanted to see if they might work better than worms. Perhaps, he thought, a bigger meal would appeal to the trout. Once again, he cast out his line with a fat night crawler on his hook. He waited for twenty minutes, but the line did not move. His patience was wearing thin, so he crouched over the bank to peek at the trout. Just like the previous time, he scared the trout and they sprinted upstream. They followed the same pattern as before, swimming up steam before returning to the spot where he had first seen them. Dean backed out, perplexed, and extremely frustrated. What was it going to take to catch at least one of these trout? Two weeks had passed, and he didn't have so much as a bite to show for his efforts.

He was becoming more obsessed than ever in his quest to catch the fish. He knew there were a lot of chubs in the stream and he had heard of fishermen catching trout using chub tails. The next afternoon he went to a section of the stream that he knew held a lot of chubs. It only took one cast before he was able to catch one of the aggressive little fish. He took the chub, cut off the tail and about half the body, and went back to try and catch one of the huge trout. He threaded the chub tail on his hook and prepared to cast the line. Blood was still draining from the chub as he cast his line blindly upstream. He didn't want to take the chance of being seen for the third time by the trout, so he stayed far from the edge of the water.

Nothing happened for about ten minutes. He was getting discouraged when suddenly, he felt the line move ever so lightly. A moment later there was a more aggressive tug on the line. He wanted so badly to set the hook, but he knew it would take a few seconds for the trout, if it really was a trout, to swallow the chub tail. Suddenly there was an extremely aggressive tug and Dean could wait no longer. It was now or never, so he jerked back on the rod and set the hook. The water exploded not ten feet from him, and the line went zinging out from the reel. The rod bent as the fish kept taking more and more line. The trout shot upstream and leaped high in the air. He hit the water with a resounding splash and took out even more line. The trout changed directions and came screaming downstream, then reversed course and headed back upstream again. This pattern repeated itself over the next ten minutes. The trout would head upstream, downstream, leap in the air creating acrobatic aerials literally doing flips before somersaulting back into the water. Dean, meanwhile, was holding on to the rod for dear life. There were seconds when Dean thought he had lost the trout. The line would occasionally go slack, and Dean would lose all hope before the trout would take off again, the line would zing, and the fight would begin anew.

After fifteen minutes the huge trout, finally exhausted, came to the surface and turned on its side. Dean had big, calloused farmer hands that he used to slip under the belly of the exhausted fish. In one quick motion he flipped the trout out of the water and up onto the bank. After so many failed attempts he had finally landed the biggest trout he had ever seen. The grin on his face told it all. He couldn't stop smiling and he couldn't wait to get home and show his family what he had caught.

Once home, the inspection of the trout began in earnest. His children had to hold the trout, feel the trout, open its mouth, touch the teeth of the trout, and of course, everyone wanted to measure the trout. The yardstick was brought out and after three attempts at an accurate measurement it was agreed by all family members that the trout measured 27 and 1/2 inches from the tip of the tail to the tip of the head.

When the trout was gutted everyone gathered around to inspect what the trout had been eating. They saw two partially digested crayfish and a black glob of digested insects.

The next morning Dean's thoughts turned to the other trout. He went back to the stream twice in the next two weeks but had no luck. He tried another chub tail thinking twice would be a charm, but he never got a hit. The next time he went to the stream, he once again spooked the trout and watched as the fish zoomed upstream. Almost immediately, the trout flashed back downstream and nervously settled into the same spot he had always occupied.

Dean went home more than a little dejected. Maybe catching the second trout wasn't in the cards. The summer was waning, and he knew he had only a few more chances to land the second trout. The tobacco crop was just about ready to be harvested, his kids were heading back to school, and there were always chores to do around the farm in addition to his regular job. He was feeling guilty about spending so many hours chasing after a trout, but he decided he would give it one last try before giving up.

The one thing he kept remembering about the trout was that once spooked they always zipped upstream and then, just as quickly, flashed back downstream to the same spot. With this thought in mind, he came up with an unusual and perhaps foolhardy idea. He had a large dip net that had been hanging in the barn for years. He inspected it to see if the netting had rotted but found it to still be serviceable. He loaded it in his car and set off for the stream. He planned on getting to the stream just before dark. There was no pretense this time. He walked up to the bank where the trout was sure to see him. The trout took off upstream just as it had done before. Dean jumped into the stream with his trousers on and placed the long-handled dip net at the angle he thought the trout usually took when coming back downstream. Within a few precious seconds he saw a wake of water coming towards him. He braced himself and had a steady hand on the dip net as darkness descended on the stream. Dean didn't see the trout, but he felt the pull as the trout hit the back of the net. Dean lifted the dip net as the trout thrashed and turned in the net.

Dean waded to shore and set the net, with the trout inside, up onto the stream bank. He had come up with an unorthodox method of capturing the trout and it had worked. When he got home, the ritual of inspecting the trout began anew. This second trout was even larger than the first. It measured just a fraction under 29 inches.

Neither of the trout went to waste. Like she had done with the first trout, his wife cut the trout into sections and fried the trout for supper along with potatoes from the garden, fresh tomatoes, and cut up watermelon slices for dessert.

If anybody knew how he had caught the trout, they might have looked askance at his method, but he had a family to feed and that took priority. He was supplying another meal for his family along with memories of catching the two largest trout he had ever encountered. That was enough for him.

Dean never went trout fishing again. He knew he would never catch another trout to equal the size of the two he had caught that summer, so, he reasoned, why try.

In time, his kids grew up and moved off the farm to find their own way in the world. Dean continued to work for the county until he retired, driving the grader five days a week maintaining the gravel roads for the county.

He lived to the ripe old age of 97. Before he passed, one of his great grandkids asked him if he would tell the story of the two giant trout that he caught that summer so many years ago. He pulled his great grandson onto his lap and told the story, gladly.

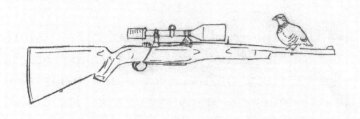

PETE THE PARTRIDGE

LeRoy Finch went out to inspect his land. He did this on a regular basis much to the chagrin of his very understanding wife. He owned three different parcels of land totaling just over 180 acres. Each parcel was purchased only after multiple inspections. He never purchased land that had been put on the market unless he was convinced the land contained the one thing he valued most. Every parcel of land he purchased had to hold deer, lots and lots of deer.

He hired a local man who was a good bulldozer operator to put in crude roads on the rugged hillsides. He needed the roads to navigate his land with his ATV. He had the same man put in field ponds wherever the terrain allowed for the collection of rainwater. Once a mud base had firmed up the bottom of the pond allowing it to hold water, he would check the ponds periodically to see how many deer had been using the pond. If the pond consistently had multiple deer using the ponds for drinking purposes, he would build a deer stand in a nearby tree that allowed for a good shooting lane. He would lop off any small branches that might deflect his arrow or rifle shell from its intended target.

He stored this information on a note pad about each pond when deciding where and when to hunt. He posted field cameras near each prospective pond at crossing points where deer most often entered the pond.

He planted food plots in valleys to attract deer, cultivated them, and regularly checked to see if the deer were using the plots as a food source on a regular basis.

He spent his summers building additional tree stands, carrying lumber on his ATV, sweating, swatting mosquitoes, and checking his body after his evening shower for ticks that might carry Lyme disease. He had known the misery of Lyme disease on three different occasions. The disease would remain in his joints for the rest of his life. All the work, sweating, grunting, hauling wood for tree stands and clearing branches were all part of summer preparations to ensure the best deer hunt possible. He waited patiently for the nights to cool, the foliage to color and create a carpet on the forest floor. This is what he lived for. Deer hunting was his passion, his obsession, and his love.

He felt lucky to live in Wisconsin, a state that held an enormous herd of white tail deer. The deer grew large and fat on farmer's oats, soybeans, and corn. In good years, acorns lay in abundance under oak trees that had shed them. A good crop of acorns would help the state's deer population survive another long winter. If the winter wasn't severe with unusual amounts of snow and cold, pregnant does would start dropping their fawns as the snows of winter gave way to green grass chutes of spring.

Early spring would arrive in fits and starts with snowstorms one day and fifty-degree weather a few days later. Many of the newborn fawns would survive, grow, and replace the deer that were harvested each fall.

He usually hunted alone although he was generous with family and relatives who didn't have their own land to hunt on. He gladly shared the land he had worked countless hours preparing so friends and relatives could enjoy the hunting season. Although he shared his land, he preferred solitary hunts alone in the woods as shadows played out on an ever-changed landscape. He could sit on a deer stand for hours without becoming bored. He would wait patiently for the long shadows of afternoon when the deer weren't so spooky. Those late afternoon shadows, as dusk was settling over the land, would eventually entice shy deer to feel secure enough to stand and leave their bedding areas. The deer would come, tentative, taking a few cautious steps before stopping to look for signs of danger. If they didn't smell potential danger, they would start to search for food and water.

Deer were always stealthy in their approach. Their hooves made little noise as they stepped over dried leaves and twigs. The sound deer made in the woods were quite different than the sounds the ubiquitous squirrels made. Squirrels, when left alone, were much more raucous than deer. They would chase one another up and down trees, rustling leaves, scattering debris in their wake. Turkeys would scratch to uncover food from the forest floor. They were easy to hear because they never went long before clucking to announce their presence. Turkeys tended to gather in small groups as they browsed. Where there was one turkey scratching for food, there were usually more turkeys nearby.

Deer on the other hand are solitary creatures. Shy in their movements they come unannounced even to the ear of the most experienced hunter. It is the last hour of daylight that hunters wait for. It is that short period of time just as the sun is setting when deer suddenly appear as an apparition. One minute they are not in the forest and the next minute you see a shadow crossing before you.

This is the reason why deer hunting is addictive to many hunters. Deer hunters describe the last hour in the woods as shadows fall, as being one with nature.

With the generous rules governing deer harvests in his home state, it was possible to shoot multiple deer during the bow, gun and black powder seasons. The venison never went to waste. LeRoy never shot deer simply for the thrill of the kill. He ate little venison himself. He would donate his deer to anyone who was too old or infirm to hunt, or anyone who really needed the meat. He would gladly give venison to someone who had been unlucky in their hunt and hadn't bagged a deer during the season.

Many sportsmen have a passion. For some it is fishing, for others, squirrels, ducks, pheasants, or hunting rabbits become their obsession.

For LeRoy, there was no other sport that offered the adrenaline rush of drawing a bead on an unsuspecting deer. It didn't matter whether it was with a gun or bow. He would pass up many deer during the various bow and gun seasons, deer that he could have easily shot, but that wasn't the point of hunting. He didn't kill a deer just for the sake of a kill. Deer hunting to him was both a spectator sport and a participation sport. He knew when the time was right, when the deer in front of his stand was worthy of his participation, just as he knew when to pass on an easy kill of a deer standing right under his tree.

He waited patiently through the dog days of summer as the distant horizon gradually eclipsed the setting sun a few minutes earlier every few days. As the night began to cool he would rise around 5 A.M., earlier some mornings, and drive to the local gas station, grab a cup of coffee and a donut as he awaited the early morning arrivals of his "Romeo" friends, "Retired Old Men Eating Out."

As the all-male contingent shuffles in there was one unwritten rule, unspoken but acknowledged by all. No words were to be spoken to the new arrival until he had a steaming cup of coffee in front of him and taken his first sip of the morning brew. After that first sip there were few topics that were off limits. They tried unsuccessfully to avoid politics, as the group was about equally divided between Republicans and Democrats, and a few others that didn't give a damn about politics and politicians. "They are all damn crooks and pathological liars anyway," was the usual refrain. For those who loved to debate politics, arguments would rage between the merits and demerits of MSNBC and Fox news. Sometimes one of the Romeos would storm off after a heated argument but no one paid much attention. The offended party would most likely reappear within a few days and the morning banter would start up again as if an argument just a few days earlier had never occurred.

On this morning, LeRoy wasn't the first to arrive at the gas station, nor was he the last. He had been hunting for a few days with nothing to show for it except the long hours he had spent in the woods. The season was just getting underway, so his anxiety level was relatively low. After his first uninterrupted sip of morning brew, he announced to the Romeo's that he had a story to tell. He promised the story would be something they had never heard before. His friends, always up for a good story, refilled their coffee cups and settled in to hear the details.

"I've been hunting for more than 50 years and I had something happen yesterday I've never seen before."

Now he had their attention.

"Okay," said Mark Spivey, "spill the beans. What happened yesterday?"

The Romeos were all in now crowding closer to hear the story.

"Like I said, I was hunting on one of my favorite deer stands yesterday. That deer stand is just below a rock outcropping where there are a cluster of sumac scrubs. I parked my ATV and walked down to my stand. The stand is sheltered by the outcropping and is out of the wind. It offers a 180-degree view of two separate hillsides where the hills come together. I've shot a lot of deer from that stand, but yesterday there was nothing moving. I had been sitting there for three or four hours and was getting ready to call it an afternoon. Suddenly a partridge flew into a tree next to me. He wasn't up in that tree but a few seconds before he flies down and lands not five feet away from where I am sitting. I know the bird must have seen me because once he landed, he was looking directly at me.

He was not the least bit scared and you won't believe what that crazy bird did next."

"Okay," said one of the Romeos, "what did he do next?"

"Damn bird flies up and lands on my rifle," said Leroy. "I've never seen anything like it all the years I've hunted."

Pete Reynolds, the resident pseudo-intellectual of the group and self-proclaimed expert on anything and everything says in his self-patronizing way, "In my experience, what you encountered wasn't a partridge. It was a ruffed grouse."

"No," pipes in Jeff walker, "what you saw was a prairie chicken. "

That comment drew a chorus of guffaws from the Romeos. "There ain't no damn prairie chickens in Wisconsin. They only have those out west someplace, maybe Nebraska." To Jeff any state west of Wisconsin was out west someplace.

Mark Spivey was the next to join in the discussion.

"Ya, I do believe what you saw was in fact a partridge." Mark, who single-handedly managed to mangle the English language daily, refused to pronounce anything by its proper name. A partridge was never a partridge to Mark. He always pronounced it, Pat-ridge.

Pete Reynolds ego wouldn't allow him to stay silent one minute longer.

"I repeat, what you saw was a ruffed grouse, known by those of us who studied Latin extensively in our formative year as "Bonasa Umbellus".

Pete was an insufferable showoff and braggart. The Romeos noticed Pete's smile was wide with satisfaction, ready to accept compliments for his intellectual prowess.

"Well," said Leroy, "you are not factually correct." "When I got home last night, I looked on the internet and partridges are more closely related to the pheasant family than they are to ruffed grouse."

In Wisconsin we refer to ruffed grouse and partridges as the same bird, but if you really want to be technical Pete, partridges and ruffed grouse are not the same bird."

All the Romeos turned toward Pete and watched his face turn crimson.

"Well," said Pete, "You will never see that damn bird again anyway, so it doesn't make any difference what you call it."

With that comment, Pete dumped his coffee in the trash and walked out of the gas station.

"So, do you think you will ever see that partridge again," asked Mark Spivey?

"If I do, you guys will be the first to know," said LeRoy.

A few days later LeRoy was back in the same general area where he had first seen the partridge. He had parked his ATV a short distance away so he wouldn't scare any deer in the vicinity and entered the woods as quietly as he could. He settled in once he found a good site line for shooting.

Within a few minutes, he heard the fluttering of wings and looked up as a partridge dive bombed his deer stand. The partridge landed not far from his feet. This had to be the same partridge he had encountered previously. What in the world, he thought, could possess this bird to be interested in a human being?

The sound of the partridge as it fluttered its wings to make its landing made LeRoy react instinctively by raising his rifle. The bird, nonplussed, hopped forward a few steps before flying up and landing on the barrel of the rifle.

LeRoy couldn't believe what he was seeing. After he recovered from the shock of the partridge sitting on the barrel of his rifle he began to giggle. The giggle soon turned into an all-out laugh.

"Well aren't you something," he said. "If you are going to keep showing up like this, we have to come up with a name for you."

"I think I will call you Pete, Pete the Partridge."

The newly named, Pete, walked up and down the barrel of the rifle. He only stopped when he came to the bolt of the gun, turned, and walked back in the other direction.

LeRoy decided to push his luck and see if Pete would allow him to be petted. LeRoy reached out to scratch the bird on its head, but when he got close enough to touch the partridge, Pete pecked LeRoy on the fingers. Apparently, familiarity went only so far with Pete. He would allow you to look, but he would not allow you to touch.

When the late afternoon shadows crept over the landscape, LeRoy cased his gun and started to walk back towards his ATV. He thought surely Pete would fly away, but when he looked back Pete was walking a few feet behind him. The bird followed LeRoy all the way back to his ATV. Pete even followed the ATV to the edge of the woods before flying off into the undergrowth.

LeRoy didn't tell his Romeo friends anything more

about his encounter with Pete, although they never failed to ask. He was afraid they wouldn't believe him if he told them that Pete had flown onto his rifle barrel and then followed him to his ATV.

Pete became a bit of an obsession with LeRoy. He continued to hunt on his other parcels of land as the season progressed. He ended up shooting four deer, two does and two bucks. The four deer would all go to people who needed the meat. He told his Romeo friends stories of each deer kill, but he never mentioned Pete the partridge to them.

As the deer seasons wore on, he found himself drawn more and more to the deer stand behind the rock outcropping. He was seldom seated for more than 30 minutes before he would hear the ruffle of feathers and smile as Pete made one of his pin-point landings.

Pete, now completely used to LeRoy, would not only fly up and set on the hunter's rifle, but he would also now walk the whole length of the rifle and then climb up on LeRoy's shoulder and eventually he would hop up on Leroy's head. He still would not allow LeRoy to touch him. That was the one area that was still off limits. An easy truce existed between bird and man. Pete was obviously interested in LeRoy and LeRoy understood that if he touched the bird, it might be the last he ever saw of Pete.

The next time LeRoy went to the deer stand Pete arrived soon after Leroy turned off the ATV. Pete, LeRoy thought, had come to associate the sound of the ATV with the arrival of the hunter. Each day when LeRoy was done hunting Pete would dutifully follow him back to his ATV. LeRoy would start the ATV and drive very slowly to the edge of the woods. Pete would follow, either walking, flying or alighting on the ATV for a ride.

A few days later LeRoy couldn't wait to get to his deer stand because he had an idea. He had brought a camera with him to see if he could take some photos of Pete. As it turned out, Pete was more than accommodating. Not only could LeRoy snap as many photos of Pete as he wanted, but LeRoy also got the impression that Pete was posing for the photos.

LeRoy never shared the photos of Pete with his coffee shop buddies. He didn't want to come across like a Pete Reynolds, a showoff who thought he had all the answers. He wasn't completely sure his friends would believe his stories, so he kept his expanded relationship with the bird to himself.

It was now in the black powder season, the last season in which you could use a gun to shoot deer when LeRoy decided to visit Pete before the full force of winter set. He walked down to the rock outcropping which now had a layer of snow covering the ground. The first thing LeRoy noticed was disrupted snow and torn up ground. He was stunned to see tail feathers on the snow and breast feathers clinging to some nearby bushes. Something, or someone had gotten to Pete. It might have been a coyote or a bird of prey. It seemed obvious to LeRoy that something had attacked Pete and it all likelihood Pate was dead.

He went home immediately and told his wife what he had just seen. He was so distraught he told his Romeo friends about Pete's fate and showed them some of the photos he had taken of Pete during the deer season.

His Romeo friends never made light of the

attachment Leroy had for the bird, but they did pepper him with questions about the photos.

It proved to be a long cold winter. The winter months slowly crept by with copious amounts of snow piling up. Cabin fever finally drove LeRoy out of the house before the last snows had melted. He decided to look for shed racks and spent a morning combing a portion of his land. He found several smaller racks, but nothing worth taking home and displaying in his garage alongside other, more prominent mounts.

He was just about to head for home after several hours of hunting for shed racks, when something told him to swing by the rock outcropping one last time. After he arrived at the destination he looked around, spending more time than he planned, but there was nothing to see. There was only snow, barren trees, and memories. He made his way slowly back to his ATV and started it up. Just after he had engaged the engine to warm up the ATV, he saw a blur and then a whir of sound and a flash of feathers. Pete dropped from the sky like a rocket and landed on his ATV.

LeRoy was both shocked and exhilarated at the same time. Somehow Pete had survived the attack that had nearly killed him. Pete had remembered the sound of the ATV from their previous encounters and had flown in to look around.

LeRoy couldn't stop smiling.

Pete the Partridge was back.

A CHANCE ENCOUNTER

The year 1934 brought the Unites States to its knees. The U. S. was in the throes of a unparalleled Depression. It had been five long years of unemployment lines, soup kitchens, bankruptcies, and even suicides. People lined up by the hundreds in search of work, but there really wasn't any work. Factories were shuttered, businesses declared bankruptcies at a rapid rate and there had been a run on banks. People were destitute. Everyone had lost something. Some had lost everything.

It would be a full year before President Roosevelt signed the Emergency Relief Appropriation Act of 1935 on January 27. On May 6, FDR would sign Executive Order 7034 that created the Works Progress Administration. The Public Works Projects were not allowed to compete with existing businesses, but they could build bridges, roads, clean sanitation facilities and clear debris. The workers were paid between $15 and $90 per month.

Thirteen-year-old Jimmy Ross had just come from his father's garage. He had hoped to see at least one car parked in the garage which would indicate his father had a paying customer who needed work done on their car. The garage bay was empty, but Jimmy stopped in to say hello to his father. His father hadn't had any work in a week. People just weren't driving. If they needed the oil changed in their car, they did it themselves rather than paying a mechanic to do the work for them. Money was tight and jobs so scarce that people had either given up looking for work or were hunkered down trying to figure out what other options they had to feed their families.

Jimmy and his dad and mom were a close-knit family. His dad had made just enough the last couple of years to keep the garage open. He had cut the price of his labor to practically nothing. There were days when he made a dollar and days, like today, when he had no customers. Still, they were better off than some families. They owned a house and a little land. When things got tight, they made their garden a little larger and shared some of the produce with neighbors who were worse off than they were.

Jimmy had sneaked his shoe-shine kit out of the house that morning and stashed it before going to his father's garage. There wasn't much call for shining shoes in town. The most he ever got was a nickel or a dime if he had done a really good job, but every penny he made was turned over to his mother.

After the short conversation with his dad, he spent an hour on a street corner trying to drum up business shining shoes. There were no takers. He decided to take a walk down by the stream that ran along the western edge of town. He had picked up a stick and was whacking at tall grass pretending he was a Chuck Klein, the Hoosier Hammer. Klein was the 1933 Phillies baseball player who won the triple crown with a .368 batting average, 28 homers, and 126 RBIs. It was a hot summer day in July and tiny tributaries of sweat were slithered like snakes down Jimmy's face and arms.

He was just about to take another whack at some weeds when he looked up and saw the car. He was the son of a garage owner, so he knew more about cars than almost anyone his age. His father would come home in the evenings and talk about cars he worked on and Jimmy would ask questions about which makes and models his dad thought were the best. Jimmy was almost certain the car he was looking at was a new 1934 Packard Twelve Sport Phaeton LeBaron. Jimmy was sure his father had shown him a picture of a Phaeton, one of the most sought-after luxury cars of 1934, but Jimmy had certainly never seen any luxury automobile like this around his small town.

Jimmy had been gazing at the car for a long time before he noticed the fisherman. The man was standing by the stream in waders putting together a fishing pole. He watched the man affix one section of the pole to the next until it reached about eight feet in length. The man attached a reel to the end of the pole and threaded line through metal brackets. The man opened a small box and took out an object that was too small for Jimmy to see. The man tied the small object to the end of the line. He walked out into the water until he was nearly up to his waist. He pulled out some excess line and did some false casts. Jimmy watched mesmerized as the pole flexed and bent with each false cast. The fisherman's hands barely moved as the line grew longer and straighter. Jimmy noticed the beautiful motion of the line with each cast until the man snapped his wrist ever so slightly and the line shot out forty feet over the water before settling gently with a tiny ripple in a still pool. Jimmy moved closer to the water until he could see the object the man had tied on his line was a fly. The fly floating on the water for only a few seconds before it was sucked under by a large brown trout. The man fought the trout as the pole bent and the trout made a long run upstream. In a few minutes, the man had the trout subdued. After removing the fly from the edge of the trout's mouth the fisherman quickly released the fish back into the water. The boy watched in amazement as the fly fisherman repeated the same process a dozen times over the next hour.

The fisherman, who had been watching the boy between casts, finally came ashore. "Are you a fisherman," asked the man?

"I like to fish," said the boy. "My father has taken me a few times, but we just take cane poles and use bobbers. We only use worms for bait. We catch a few, but we always take them home to eat. Why do you throw yours back?"

"Well," said the man, "A meal of trout occasionally makes for some fine eating, but if I throw them back, I might catch them again another day."

"I guess," said Jimmy, "but folks are having tough times, so they'd eat any trout they catch. That's a mighty fine-looking pole you got mister. I've never seen anything like it. What's it called?"

"I brought two fly rods with me. The British would call them split cane rods, but we Americans call them split bamboo fly rods. They are made by splitting sections of bamboo into six-sided hexagon patterns. The men who make these rods are true artists. The bamboo is measured every few inches to get a perfect taper to the rod. The guides are wrapped with silk thread and the rod is varnished to an exceptionally fine sheen. One of these rods was made by H. L. Leonard and the other one is a H. S. Gillum rod. The cork grips alone can take up to forty hours of labor to complete. I store them in a cool place when I'm not fishing, and I take each section apart."

"I bet they are expensive," said the boy, "but not as expensive as that car. What a beauty."

"My name is Joe, Joseph Stapleton, but my friends call me Joe," said the man with a smile.

"I'm Jimmy, Jimmy Ross. Everybody just calls me Jimmy. That's a '34 Packard Twelve Sport Phaeton by LeBaron isn't it? My dad runs a garage here and he says your '34 Packard is the finest car made this year."

"I like it," said Joe, "but it's just a car, and those expensive fly rods are just fly rods. It's people who are important."

"I agree," said Jimmy. "My parents don't have much money being the Depression and all, but they treat me great. I couldn't ask for better parents."

"How old are you, Jimmy?"

"I'm thirteen."

"Well, Jimmy, I consider myself to be a pretty good judge of character, and I'd judge you to be a very mature thirteen-year-old."

"Thank you, sir. I appreciate that."

"Say, I'm going to be here for a week. I needed to get out of the city and there is no better way of doing that than taking a side trip to fish for trout. It is one of my favorite pastimes, and unfortunately, I don't get many opportunities to do it. I do have one small problem though. I don't know the streams around here. Since you are local, I bet you know the best streams in the area. Would you be interested in being my guide for a week? We would be fishing from early morning until sundown with a break for lunch. I'll pay you a decent wage for your services when the week is done."

"Well, sir, I'd have to ask my parents first, and you'd have to come by and meet them. If they say it's okay, I'd very much like to do that. My dad's garage is right around the corner. Can we go ask him now?"

"No time like the present," said Joe.

They drove up in the Packard with Jimmy riding in the passenger's seat. Sam noticed the car first, before he saw his son riding in the luxury automobile. He put down a rag he had been using to clean up an oil spill and came out to see his son and meet the stranger in the expensive car.

"Mighty fine car you got there, mister," said Sam Ross. "First one I've seen in person. You won't find another like that in these parts."

Joe got out of the car and introduced himself to Sam. He explained the encounter of meeting Jimmy on the stream and the positive impression the boy had made on him. He recounted the story of being here for a week of fly fishing, staying at the local hotel, and his plan of fishing for trout every day. He'd like to hire Jimmy as his guide if that was amenable to his father. He'd like Jimmy to take him around to local streams and would pay him at the end of the week for doing so.

Sam said he would have to talk the arrangement over with his wife. He gave Joe their address near the edge of town and they agreed to meet at seven the next morning. If it was okay with his wife, then Jimmy could guide him to the local streams. School was out for the summer and it would be good for the boy to be able to make a little spending money.

After a short conversation between Joe and Sam about the mechanical pluses and minuses of the new Packard, Joe left to go back to the hotel. Joe had been impressed that neither Sam nor Jimmy had mentioned anything about money.

When Sam got home his wife met him at the door and told him that Jimmy had already been pleading his case with her for an hour. Wouldn't she, "Please. Pretty, pretty, please," allow him this opportunity to guide the fisherman with the fancy car?

Sam and his wife, Claire, talked about the offer over supper. Claire wasn't too keen on the idea. After all they didn't know this stranger. Jimmy kept quiet; this was adult conversation, and his comments weren't welcome. Instead, he cleared the dishes, starting with his mother's first, and began to wash them so he could overhear his parent's discussions. Claire tried not to smile but she couldn't help herself. In the end, she relented with the misgivings of a mother concerned about the safety of her only child.

"You can go," she said, "as long as I can talk to the man in the morning."

Jimmy went to bed, tossing and turning before finally drifting off to sleep. He was awake by six the next morning, washed up, dressed and downstairs a half hour later. He waited by the window until the Packard showed up a few minutes after seven.

Joe got out of his car and Jimmy was out the door in a flash escorting him into the house to meet his mother. Joe, seeming to sense the hesitation on the part of Jimmy's mother, extended his hand, made small talk, accepted a cup of coffee, and asked about her family before expressing how impressed he had been with his chance encounter with Jimmy.

Jimmy breathed a huge sigh of relief when his mom said, "Okay, you'd best be on your way. The sun is up, and I imagine there are trout to be caught." She gave Jimmy a hug, and said, "I'll see you this evening."

She had one last word for Joe. "This is a good opportunity for Jimmy. Just make sure you take good care of my boy. He's the only one I have."

"Yes, Ma'am," said Joe. "I'll watch over him like he was my own son."

Claire wasn't sure, but she thought she saw a little moisture at the edges of Joe's eyes with those words.

Once they were in the car and pulling out of the driveway, Joe said, "You are the guide now, so you take the lead. Where are we headed?"

"I thought we should go to Tainter Creek first. It's a small little creek, but there are a lot of trout in the stream if you can catch them."

Joe smiled at the comment. "You show me the stream and I'll catch the trout."

Thirty minutes later they were parked by the stream and Joe had the 8-foot H. L. Leonard bamboo fly rod all assembled and ready to cast. There didn't appear to be anyone else on the stream.

The stream itself had a series of riffles and some long pools of quiet water. On his third cast Joe hooked a nice brown trout that made several runs up the riffles before it was subdued and netted. Six casts later he caught a little seven-inch brown trout, and five more casts produced a ten-inch brook trout with skin as soft as velvet.

They fished for three hours and Joe caught fifteen trout and had lost five or six others. Jimmy was mesmerized by the casting and Joe took time to explain how to cast a line over the water so it would only make a tiny ripple when it landed and not scare the trout. Joe demonstrated how to make a series of different casts and explained why they were useful. Jimmy was fascinated with all the information and it didn't seem to bother Joe in the least that he asked so many questions. In fact, Joe seemed to thoroughly enjoy the questions. He laughed a lot when he lost a trout, chastising himself for being such a lousy fly fisherman. Jimmy couldn't help but smile at Joe's absurd comment about his fishing ability. It was obvious to this thirteen-year-old boy that he was in the presence of an excellent fly fisherman.

They stopped around noon and sat in the shade of a tree to eat a lunch that had been packed by the hotel. Joe had caught twenty-three trout by Jimmy's count, including an eighteen-inch brown that had put up a hard fight, repeatedly jumping high out of the water, making long runs before finally being subdued. After each catch Joe quickly removed the fly from the trout and released it back into the water. He explained that trout are fragile fish out of water. They can't breathe, are often exhausted from the fight, and they might very well die if not quickly placed back into their natural environment. "We are here to catch them, Jimmy, not to kill them."

Jimmy's curiosity was endless, taking in all the information Joe had to offer, getting more and more intrigued with this information about fly fishing, fly rods, and the different varieties of flies. He learned there were dry flies, wet flies and nymphs, soft hackle flies, emerger flies, tiny flies that were hard to see on the water and big streamer patterns fished subsurface. Each had a purpose depending on the time of year and what hatches were coming off the water on any given day.

"Do you know what the most perfect fly in the world is, Jimmy?"

"No, sir."

"The perfect fly, Jimmy, is the one that is working best on any given day. Every fly has its day. If there is a caddis hatch coming off, then you don't need another fly. Trout will gobble up that fly every time and bypass all others."

"That was a really good lunch, but I'm not quite ready to get back in the water. I think it is time for you to learn how to cast a line. Grab that Leonard rod you've been carrying. I've got an extra reel in my vest and we will get you all rigged up in just a few minutes."

Jimmy practiced for the next half hour on a grassy field. Joe was a patient instructor, offering tips on the back cast, feeling the slight tug as the line unfurls. The forward cast, at first was too big and loopy with the fly line plopping down in the water. They both laughed at Jimmy's miscues, but after another fifteen minutes of practice Jimmy had improved enough that Joe pronounced him ready to get in the water and try his luck.

Jimmy waded into the water in his old worn blue jeans and shoes. He was surprised how cold the water was, but excited at the prospect of trying to catch a trout. He was worried about the cost of the fly rod and what would happen if he would break it, but Joe didn't seem to give it a second thought.

Jimmy's first cast was awful. He was nervous, had a big loop in the forward cast, and the fly plunked down in the water with a splash. Jimmy looked nervously over at Joe and they both started laughing at the same time.

"Pretty awful," said Jimmy.

"You'll do better," said Joe. "Keep casting."

Jimmy did get better. After fifteen minutes Jimmy could cast a line that didn't splash down in the water, but he knew he had scared all the trout away in that initial pool, so they moved on.

The next section of the stream contained a long run with fast moving water. Joe instructed Jimmy to cast the line at the foam line that was running down the middle of the stream.

"That seam," said Joe, "will carry any insects to the trout. It's like a buffet line for trout. Hit that seam and you will get a hook up."

On the fourth cast his fly disappeared. Jimmy was so excited he jerked up on the rod and pulled the fly out of the fish's mouth. Jimmy looked at Joe, who was trying hard to suppress a laugh.

"You're doing great. Cast again, same spot."

His next cast was better, but the trout missed the fly. He had no takes on his next two casts but on his third cast a trout came right out of the water and inhaled his fly. The fly line went zinging through the water as the trout made a run that stripped line from the reel. Joe was so excited that he jumped up and down on the bank shouting encouragement to Jimmy. He didn't stop smiling until Joe landed the thirteen-inch brown.

They exchanged high fives as Jimmy held up his trout for Joe to see. There are those rare moments in life when you know something with complete certainty. Jimmy knew the moment he landed the brown trout that he was hooked on fly fishing and would be for the rest of his life.

They spent the rest of the afternoon walking along the meandering stream. A hatch of small mayflies started coming off the water at three in the afternoon. Joe switched flies, tying on a small Adams dry fly. The fishing was fast and furious for an hour until the hatch started to peter out. Joe caught 22 trout during that hour including two large brown trout that were both over 20 inches in length.

Joe returned Jimmy to his parent's house by seven that night just as he had promised. There was still time to fish, the sun low, shadows creeping across the water, but Joe wanted to get Jimmy home before darkness set in. Joe had enjoyed the day with Jimmy immensely, and he didn't want to get him home any later and get on the wrong side of Jimmy's mother.

Plans were made for the next day before Joe returned to the hotel, ordered a big steak and a nice glass of wine. He couldn't remember a day when he had so much fun. At first, he couldn't quite put his finger on why that was. He had fished the great streams of the west, hired top guides and paid handsomely for it, but nothing compared to having this novice boy by his side and seeing him land his first trout with a fly rod.

The next few days fell into a steady rhythm. He would pick Jimmy up by seven and they would set off to find a new stream to fish. They would fish hard in the morning with Joe doing all the fishing while Jimmy carried the extra fly rod and supplies. After lunch Joe would continue his tutelage with Jimmy on the art of fly fishing. He would turn over rocks in the stream and explain the entomology of insects. He instructed Jimmy on the use of roll casts, reach casts, false casts and steeple casts. He showed Jimmy how to do a double haul cast to increase the distance of a cast.

Joe never criticized when Jimmy made mistakes. He would explain the mistake that Jimmy had made and how to correct it while always encouraging and complimenting when Jimmy learned a new skill. Joe couldn't remember when he had ever had so much fun. He loved being the teacher and Jimmy was turning into a sponge as a student. Jimmy continuously asked questions and practiced until he was at least somewhat proficient, listening intently to instructions.

Joe became less interested in his own fishing and more interested in teaching this intelligent, inquisitive, hardworking boy.

The second day they fished a small tributary stream that eventually flowed into a larger stream. The plan was to fish the small stream for a few hours before switching to the larger stream. The small stream turned out to be chock full of trout. They weren't big trout, but they would come to the fly easily. Sometimes there were three or four trout chasing the fly at the same time.

After an early lunch, Joe insisted Jimmy try the H. L. Leonard fly rod. "Try the Leonard. See how it compares to the Gillum."

The afternoon fishing was terrific. Joe insisted they switch off fishing after each stretch of new water. The fishing was mostly in pocket water with occasional riffles and slow meandering runs. By the end of the day Joe said, "I have no idea how many trout we caught."

"I know exactly how many," said Jimmy. "You caught 83 trout and I caught 21. What a day. I never thought I'd ever catch that many trout. This is the most fun I have ever had."

Not as much as me, thought Joe. Not as much as me.

The next day brought a small shower in the morning followed by light drizzle. The stream they had planned on fishing was brown with runoff.

"Doesn't look good," said Jimmy. "I'm really sorry about that."

"Not your fault," replied Joe. "Gives me a good chance to show you how to fish with nymphs.

Joe tied on a prince nymph and cast a line within a few inches of the far bank. The current swirled and a bow began to appear in the line. Joe simply lifted the line, turned his wrist upstream, and placed the line down again, mending the line and taking the bow out while maintaining a natural drift.

"Okay, your turn," said Joe.

The first few times Jimmy tried to mend the line he failed miserably. Joe, ever the patient teacher, instructed, encouraged, and sometimes demonstrated until Jimmy gradually got the hang of mending the line against the current.

They decided to move on to a smaller stream that might clear up by noon and allow them the opportunity to fish with nymphs.

Joe only fished for an hour, catching five fish before turning the fishing duties over to Jimmy. Funny, he thought, I came here for a week of fishing but I'm having much more fun teaching this kid how to use a fly rod.

Every hour he had Jimmy switch from the Leonard fly rod to the Gillum rod while peppering Jimmy with questions on how he thought each rod responded.

Just as shadows were descending over the water, making it difficult to see the fly line, Jimmy felt the line tighten. He lifted the rod, felt the take, and watched as the water exploded. The fly line went singing through the water as the trout kept taking more and more line from the reel.

"Keep the rod tip up," said Joe. "That's a really big trout."

The tussle between fisherman and fish seemed to last forever. There were runs and leaps by the trout until Jimmy finally nudged the fish closer to shore. Just as Jimmy thought the trout close enough to be landed, the fish would take off on another run. After the fifth run, the trout finally turned on its side as Joe reached down with his landing net and scooped up the brown trout.

The trout was so big that that its tail and part of its

head hung out of the landing net. Jimmy's hands were shaking so badly it took him some time to look up at Joe. What he saw was the broad smile on Joe's face.

"That was one terrific fight," said Joe. "You are fast becoming one fine trout fisherman."

Joe pulled out a tape measure and the trout measured 29 ½ inches from tail to the tip of the mouth. It was a male brown trout with a large hooked lower jaw.

"Better put him back in the water," said Joe. "He will help produce a lot of offspring this fall."

Jimmy held the huge trout by its tail and swished water through the gills until it was strong enough to make a strong push with its tail and glide into the dark water.

Joe dropped Jimmy off at his house before driving to the hotel. As much as he had enjoyed the day and watching Jimmy catch the trout of a lifetime, he couldn't get over his growing sense of melancholy. It took him until trying to drop off to sleep that night before acknowledging his melancholy was due to the realization that he only had two days left of fishing with Jimmy.

It took him an hour of tossing and turning before he was able to fall into a fitful sleep.

The next two days went by in a flash. They fished two different streams. The trout were active and not particularly picky. If you presented a fly in a delicate manner and got a half-way decent drift the trout would flash to the fly, the rod would bend, and the fight would be on.

On the last day of fishing, Jimmy caught almost as many trout as Joe. Gosh, thought Joe, the kid is getting good.

Before dropping Jimmy off at his house, he asked if Jimmy could stop by the hotel the next day. "Don't come by before noon. I will probably be sleeping in late."

Just as Jimmy was getting out of the car, Joe said, "Just out of curiosity, which one of the fly rods did you enjoy the most?"

"Wow," said Jimmy, "that is a hard one." "Both rods are great. They really are pieces of art."

He thought about it for several minutes before replying. "If I had to choose, I guess I'd choose the Gillum, but both are great fly rods. You couldn't go wrong with either one."

The next day Jimmy was at the hotel by one o'clock. Joe wasn't in the lobby, so he searched out Mike Burrows, the hotel owner.

"I'm looking for Joe," said Jimmy. "Is he still sleeping?"

"Why, no," said Mike, "he left at seven this morning. He said he wanted to get an early start on his trip home. He left a wake-up call for 6 a.m."

Mike noticed a tear slide down Jimmy's cheek.

"He did leave a package for you, though. Made me promise to give it to you when you showed up. He was real particular about that. Make sure the boy gets this," he said.

Mike handed Jimmy a large package tied up with string.

Jimmy untied the strings and opened the package. The first thing he saw was an envelope with his name on it. He ripped open the envelope and saw the note inside. $14 in one-dollar bills spilled out of the note.

This was more money than Jimmy had ever held in his hands. He had enjoyed Joe so much he had completely forgotten he was supposed to receive payment for guiding. Next, he read the words on the note.

"Dear Jimmy,

I have enjoyed this past week beyond words. I can't remember when I have had a more enjoyable time. I take many fond memories with me, not the least of which was your skill as a guide and your pleasant disposition as a companion. Your wages were fairly earned. The package I leave as a present with the hope that you will enjoy it for many years to come."

He signed it, "Your friend, Joe."

Jimmy ripped open the package and gazed in wonder at the four-piece bamboo fly rod, reel, creel, and three dozen flies. He recognized the fly rod immediately. It was the Gillum, the fly rod he said was his favorite. Now he understood why Joe had asked him to compare the two fly rods. It had been Joe's intention to give him the fly rod that Jimmy most preferred.

Jimmy left the hotel without another word. His hands were shaking, and tears were trickling down his face as he made his way back home.

A week later Jimmy's parents received a letter in the mail. Inside was a note which read: "I can't express to you how grateful I am for allowing Jimmy to be my guide on my recent fly-fishing trip to your beautiful driftless area. Not only was Jimmy a terrific guide with a winning personality, but he also taught me how to enjoy life again even in these trying times."

"Enclosed is a check to put towards a college fund for Jimmy. Please don't tell him I sent this money. I'd advise not putting the money in the bank at the present time. Better days will come, and you can deposit the money when banks and the economy stabilize."

When Jimmy's parents looked at the check, they couldn't believe all the zeros they were seeing. The check was made out for the astounding sum of $1,500.00.

Jimmy's parents knew the money they had just received would be more than enough to pay for a fine college education for their son.

They noticed the heading printed on the check: Joseph Stapleton III, President, LeBaron Motor Works.

Sixty Years Later:

The fisherman let the car drift off the shoulder of the gravel road and come to rest under the shade of a maple tree. The car, like the man, was old. The paint was faded from too many years in the sun. There had once been air conditioning in the car, but that had gone out nearly ten years ago. It would have cost more to repair the air conditioning than the car was worth. Of course, in hindsight, that wasn't true, but who knew then that the car would hold together for another ten years. The car burned a little oil, sometimes coughing and sputtering before firing. He only used it for short trips, not trusting it to go into the city. He had a newer car, but he seldom felt the need to use it. His two daughters picked up anything he needed when they went to the city and he felt no worse for avoiding the traffic, the congestion, and the people who caused it. When you are seventy-four years old, you do things that please you and beg off those that don't.

What the old man was doing today was one of the things that pleased him; had pleased him for the past sixty years. He was going trout fishing.

He thought for a minute, reminiscing about where the past sixty years had taken him. He had graduated high school and gone off to college. It would be years before he would learn where the money had come from to fund that education. He had majored in entomology and been drafted into the army upon graduation. He served two years in Europe fighting the Nazi's, was decorated for valor in combat and returned home without telling anyone what he had seen or done while fighting for his country.

He went back to school on the G. I. Bill obtaining a master's degree and eventually a doctorate. He worked at the local college only twenty miles from where he grew up. He taught a two-week interim class each spring. The class was called, "Introduction to Fly Fishing." The class was only open to ten students. The only criteria were, you had to be a novice, someone who had never fished before. Each student had to submit an essay on why they should be chosen for the class. He taught the ten students how to cast a fly line, stream etiquette, and in each session, students had to turn over rocks in the stream and identify various nymphalid forms that lived in the streams.

The two-week course was Pass/Fail. In order to pass the class, you had to hook and land a trout. In all the years he taught the course, he had never had a student fail the two-week class. He was patient yet demanding. His students affectionately called him, "Dr. Bug."

He had married twice and loved once. He had met

Edy Schmits shortly before being drafted. They had gone on only one date, but that was all it took for him to be smitten. Somehow, he knew this was the woman he was going to marry. She felt the same way and told him not to die in the war before she could marry him.

After Jim came back from the war, they did marry. Together they raised two daughters and no sons. They were married twenty-eight years and then she was gone. The doctor diagnosed Edy with ovarian cancer and she passed away four months later.

Jim had no desire to re-marry, but after six years his daughters set him up on a blind date, saying, "Dad, it's time you got back in the game."

He married Jeannie Morris six months later and the marriage never worked. Jeannie was a perfectly fine woman, but they literally had nothing in common. She preferred dinners at nice restaurants while he liked a burger and a beer at the local bar. She liked to travel to exotic locations while he preferred small town life. She tolerated his long hours fly fishing, but felt he spent too much time on fishing and not enough time on her.

They separated as friends after three years of marriage. They still talked on the phone at least once a month and exchanged birthday and Christmas cards each year. His two daughters never tried to encourage him to date again.

He thought about all these things as he eased himself out of his car. He thought about Joe, dead and gone all these years ago. He had so many memories to look back on over his lifetime. He had seen presidents come and go. Some in grace, some in disgrace, and some in coffins. He thought about the son he never had. There would be no son to follow him down to this stream. No son to impart his wisdom to about fly fishing. No son to show the beauty of a trout rising to a dry fly. No son to watch as a hatch of thousands of caddis flies come off the water as trout greedily gulped them down. No son to understand the cycle of the fishing year. Nymphs first, then dry flies, streamers, and midges. No son to show how to tie flies when the snow was three feet deep as you prepared for the cycle to begin again.

He had few regrets in life. Not having a son to go along with two daughters was his only real regret, but of course he never mentioned that to his daughters whom he loved dearly. He regretted marrying Jeannie Morris. He should have told her from the start that he could only love once. He would take that guilt of omission to his grave.

He thought of his lifelong love of trout fishing and how it had changed over the past sixty years. Some things, he had to admit, were better now, but some were worse. Equipment was much better. Graphite rods were better, fly line and leaders were all better. Environmental laws were better. Catch and release which most fly fishermen now used was much better. On the other hand, the trout were smaller now and he didn't have much time for a lot of the new age fly fishermen in their breathable waders, fancy vests, and their numerous fly boxes that carried a hundred varieties of flies. They didn't seem to understand that presentation of the fly is much more important than the fly you choose. Of course, they hadn't had a lifetime to learn that lesson, or myriad other lessons, and they didn't seem interested in asking someone who did.

He thought of all these things as he eased himself out of his car. He enjoyed the sun on his brow as he opened his trunk and took out his boots and his old fishing vest. The zipper on his vest hadn't worked in years. He used two large safety pins to keep it closed. He picked up his hat that was as faded as the vest and headed back to the car to dress. He sat on the car seat with the door open, the sun shining in and a slight breeze in his face. He removed his shoes and slowly eased into his boots and tugged hard to get his feet securely to the bottom. He stood and eased the vest on and then the hat and sunglasses. He pulled the reel from its case and prepared to affix it to the rod.

Finally, there was only one more thing to do.

He undid the string on his rod case. He slowly slid out a four-piece bamboo rod and began to assemble it. It was an incredibly old rod. It was a rod that had caught countless trout. It was a rod that could perhaps catch more trout today. He had new guides put on the rod some years ago and had the rod stripped and new varnish reapplied by a craftsman who specialized in old, expensive fly rods.

The one thing that had not changed in all these years was the name on the side of the rod. In clear distinct lettering was written the name, H. S. Gillum.

It was a rod from so many years ago. A rod with so many stories to tell and so little time to tell them.

Jim affixed the reel to the rod and screwed it on tight. He pulled the leader through the guides and tied on an Adams dry fly.

He took one last look inside the car to make sure he had everything he needed and slowly moved off toward the waiting water.

TAKING CHASE HOME

Robert Miller III grew up knowing full well how lucky he was to be born into a wealthy family that practiced law for a living. With his family's wealth he never had to worry about applying for a part time job, the cost of a pair of shoes, or how much insurance he should carry on the new car his family gave him for his sixteenth birthday. If he got top grades, there was always a healthy allowance that allowed him to take his latest girlfriend out for dinner and a movie. He was bright and well-liked by fellow students at the prestigious private school he attended. The school offered a well-rounded education and the academic credentials that would assure he would be accepted to one of the finest universities on the eastern seaboard.

Once he obtained his undergraduate degree, he was accepted into the graduate program of a top tier law school. As he started his graduate program, he discovered that he had a skill set for the more complex and arcane aspects of tax law.

He graduated Summa Cum Laude at 24 and was soon offered a job at a prominent law firm where he quickly established himself as a rising star. He married his college sweetheart two years later and they purchased a nice condo not far from work.

He made the hours count, rather than counting the hours, and within a few years he was making the law firm so much money that there was talk from senior partners that Robert might be the youngest lawyer to make partner sometime in the not-too-distant future.

Thoughts of children, that both he and his wife said they wanted, kept getting pushed forward to some unknown future date. He knew with the crazy hours he was booking each week that he would be an absentee father, so he kept on working, and put parenthood on hold.

As his client base grew, he worked more and more with the super wealthy, titans of industry, movie stars and professional athletes. Some were nice, but most he found to be both snobbish and demanding. They had more money than they could ever spend, but they were still greedy for more. They demanded more of his time and more of his expertise so they might legally pay the smallest amount in taxes. Robert's legal expertise allowed them to do exactly that.

One year turned into the next and by the time

Robert turned 50 he made partner and commanded a yearly salary well north of seven figures. He still worked crazy hours and the only vacation he and his wife took was two weeks in Barbados each summer. He knew he was getting burned out with the endless hours and the petty clients that were never satisfied with their tax returns.

He came home one day to find his wife in tears. She had gone in for her annual mammogram and the doctor did not like what she saw. A follow-up appointment only confirmed what the doctor already suspected.

She underwent chemotherapy, lost all her hair, vomited daily, and died six months later.

For the first time in his life, Robert was completely alone. He was alone with his thoughts, angry at himself to the point of self-loathing. He was angry at missing out on anniversaries, birthdays and the lost time with his wife that he could never get back. He was angry about children that were never conceived and their laughter he would never hear.

Days turned into weeks. His partners called frequently telling him to take all the time he needed; they understood his present circumstances.

After he was gone a month, the partners called to gently tell him it was time to come back to work. He was an income producing rainmaker for the firm and that trumped everything else. Clients were calling. They demanded time with Robert. They weren't pleasant in their demands.

He got up on a Monday and shaved for the first time in a week. He put on his last clean shirt and a decent suit. As Robert arrived at the office building, he took the elevator up to the seventh floor carrying only a cardboard box and an envelope.

Word spread quickly that Robert was in the office. The senior partners were some of the first to come out of their offices and welcome him back. He handed them the envelope and walked into his office and started putting a few framed photos in the box. This, he thought, is all that is left after almost thirty years of working for this firm.

The partners, having digested the content of the resignation letter, tried to talk him out of leaving. The only words he spoke when he left the building were, "I'm done. I'm no different from those egotistical idiots I represented. I traded all the things that are important in life—time, family, and happiness—for money."

He took the elevator down to the ground floor and promised himself he would never look back.

Several months of depression passed at a glacial pace until one day, out of boredom, he turned on his computer. He remembered a client who had mentioned how much he had enjoyed a vacation in the driftless area of Wisconsin. Robert spent the next three hours looking at maps, aerial views, houses and property in the driftless area of southwestern Wisconsin. He spent the next few days scanning his computer while becoming fascinated with the beauty of the farmland, escarpments, rolling hills, streams and hard wood forests that made up the driftless region.

The next day he called a realtor and put his condo up for sale. The realtor agreed to sell the condo with the expensive furnishings for an exorbitant fee. With that decision out of the way, he packed two bags and bought a one-way plane ticket to Madison, Wisconsin.

He had booked a window seat on the flight. The sky was clear as he looked out over well-groomed farm fields planted with corn, soybeans, and wheat. He got a bird's eye view of marshes, rivers and small creeks, as well as his first glimpses of the Mississippi River, a giant serpent slithering through high limestone bluffs.

He marveled at the beauty of the hills and valleys, and timber, so much timber everywhere.

As he sat looking out the plane's window, it struck him that this could be the place where he might spend the rest of his life.

He took a taxi from the airport to a hotel, stayed overnight, and then took another taxi to a downtown car dealership. He bought a new pickup even though he had never owned or driven one before. Something just told him that this was the kind of vehicle he would need. He paid full price for the vehicle with his platinum credit card without bothering to dicker on the price.

He put his two bags in the cab of the truck, stopped only long enough to buy a cup of coffee, a Wisconsin road map, and hit the road.

He spent the next three days driving rural roads as he tried to orient himself with the countryside. He talked to three different realtors and explained in detail what he was looking for. He spent each night in small motels and ate at local diners. He was a good listener from time spent as a lawyer and he overheard conversations about the weather, local politics, the price of soybeans, wedding plans of an excited young couple and debates on whether the Packers were going to beat the Chicago Bears in the upcoming season.

The conversations he heard focused on small town, rural life, but he found that refreshing. There was no talk about tax shelters, offshore accounts, and owning multiple homes in states that offered tax incentives. After spending much of his previous life around pompous blowhards, it felt good to be around salt of the earth folks. He couldn't wait to fit in. As he got up to leave the local restaurant, he left a ten-dollar tip for a seven-dollar breakfast, got back in his truck, and drove.

On the fifth day he bought a farm.

He noticed a sign as he drove into yet another small town. The sign read, "Welcome to Bradford, home of the Mighty Braves, population 677 and still growing strong. Come as a visitor and stay as a friend."

He drove around the downtown, what there was of it. There were two gas stations, a family restaurant with a sign in the window that read, "Home of the Bagel Burger." There was a small grocery store, barber shop, two beauty salons, and a high school with a wooden statue of an Indian that looked like it had been carved with a chain saw. He assumed the Indian must be the Mighty Brave.

He noticed a realty sign with photos in the window of houses for sale. He pulled into a parking spot and was looking at photos of some of the houses when an attractive woman stuck her head out the door and said, "Don't just stand there gawking, come on in and gawk."

"Hi, I'm Betty Flanders. Born and raised here, lived here all my life, and I know every inch of this county. "If yu'r lookin' for something to buy, I'm the gal who can find it for you."

He smiled at her relaxed manner and explained that he was looking to purchase some land, with or without a house. If the land didn't have a house, he might want to have a house built to his specifications.

"How much land are you looking for," said Betty?

"Quite a bit of land, but it must have some fields, some good pockets of timber, and it would be better if it had a stream or some type of water on the property."

"Well, isn't this your lucky day. I just happen to have the place for you. The old Baxter place just came up for sale. It's 130 acres with some fields, quite a bit of timber, and a small stream."

"When could I see it?"

"Hop in my jeep and we will take a run out there right now. It's only a couple miles outside of town as the crow flies."

"As the crow flies? I don't believe I'm familiar with that expression."

"Oh, it's just a local expression. You'll get used to it if you end up living here."

They walked the land at a leisurely pace stopping frequently to chat or point out some feature of the property. Robert loved it and with each step he took he became more and more convinced that he didn't need to look any further. He had found what he had been looking for.

They drove back to Betty's office enjoying the silence. Betty poured Robert another cup of coffee as they casually talked about the property. Robert appreciated Betty not bothering to give him the hard sell, a canned speech about how many folks were interested in the property or mentioning he had better act fast before the property was gone.

When she finally got around to mentioning the price, all he said was, "Sold."

"You're not from anywhere around here, are you?"

"How did you know?"

"Well, you roll your R's for one thing, and any fool that lives in this town would bargain till all the bark was off a tree before he would pay the full price for any farm around these parts."

"A fair observation," he said with a smile. "I know what I like, and I liked this land as soon as I got out of the car. The house needs some work, but I suppose you could recommend someone."

"Sure. The Benson brothers do good work, and they work cheap. They will do a good job for you. They are local folks, and honest as the day is long."

"Now that we have settled on the price, how would you like to pay for the property?"

"Will you be taking out a loan? Our local banker is a pretty decent guy to work with."

"I'll pay cash, or I could use a credit card if that works better for you."

"Mister, there aren't three people in this town who could afford to buy that farm and there sure ain't one of them that would have a credit line to buy it with a credit card."

"When can we close?"

"How does tomorrow suit you?"

A month later the alterations on the farmhouse were complete, new furniture was brought in, and a used tractor was purchased. One of the Benson brothers gave Robert some lessons on the ins and out on how to safely operate the tractor.

Over the following weeks Robert made many trips

into town to pick up supplies. He bought "No Trespassing" signs that read, "All violators will be prosecuted." He bought fence posts, nails and a post hole digger.

He was proud of all the things he had learned in his first month as a new landowner. He had been so busy that he hadn't had time to meet many of the townspeople, but now that things had slowed down, he wanted that to change.

He started driving his truck to town each morning and parked at the local restaurant. He had learned enough in a month about local culture to realize the restaurant was the place where town gossip was bantered about over the day's first cup of coffee. He was anxious to meet the townspeople and become a part of the fabric of the community.

If he expected to be greeted with open arms, he soon became sorely disappointed. The banter, loud and raucous, would stop as soon as he was served his first cup of Joe.

Robert couldn't figure these people out. Why didn't they like him? Why were they so unfriendly? Why wouldn't they engage him in their conversations?

He began to wonder if he had made a mistake moving to a town this small. What first seemed so promising, was now beginning to wear on him.

He walked out of the restaurant, crossed the street, and went to seek out the one person who had treated him like family.

Betty Flanders was open for business and she met him at the door with a smile.

She looked at Robert and said, "Who ate your lunch?"

"What do you mean?"

"You look like some bully just stole your lunch."

"I can't figure these folks out," he said. "I'm trying to be friendly, get to know them, but they won't have anything to do with me. What the hell am I doing wrong?"

"Come sit a spell, drink a cup of my delicious coffee and I will give you a tutorial on small town life."

"First off, you might think you are like everyone else, but you aren't. You are different. You have a hell of a lot more money than these folks will see in a lifetime. Hell, the Bensons almost tripped over themselves with how much money you paid them for fixing up the farmhouse. On top of that rumor, the story has it has it you paid them a bonus for finishing the work so quickly."

"I might be the only one in town that knows you were a high-priced lawyer."

"You have to understand that people in small towns take a while to get to know someone when they first meet them. It doesn't take a rocket scientist to know you have a hell of a lot more education than these folks have ever been exposed to. You scare them. They don't know how to take you."

"Okay, I get that, but there is something else going on."

"Indeed, there is. Your biggest mistake was posting your land. Locals here hunted on that farm when the Baxter's owned it. The Baxter's would let people hunt on their farm if they asked nicely. Now they've noticed that you've posted the land and they don't like that. Let's just say they are a bit frosty around you because of that."

"I don't really care if people hunt on the farm. I just thought everyone posted their land. What do they hunt?"

"Oh, they hunted deer on the property for sure, along with turkeys, a few peasants, ruffed grouse, rabbits and squirrels. I know it is hard for you to understand coming from your city background but quite a few folks around here rely on that meat to supplement their diets. They especially need this in the winter months when work slows to a crawl.

"Look, Robert, you own the land and have every right to post it if you want to, but folks would treat you a whole lot different if you didn't post it."

Robert paused to take this information in before saying, "Thank you so much, Betty. You've been a great help."

"Anytime, Mr. Highfalutin Lawyer," she said, with a wink and a smile. "Anytime. The coffee is always on."

That afternoon Robert climbed on his tractor and removed all the posted signs. He plowed out a parking space for cars and he painted a large new sign. The sign read: ALL ARE WELCOME TO HUNT ON THIS PROPERTY. PLEASE JUST CLOSE THE GATE WHEN YOU LEAVE. He signed it simply, Rob Miller.

The next morning Stub Martin and Larry Fowler were drinking coffee when Robert walked into the coffee shop. This time the banter never stopped when he ordered his coffee. He pulled out his wallet to pay but the waitress said, "It's okay, those bums over there already paid for it."

"By the way, my name is Alice. Nice to meet you, Mr. Miller."

"Please Alice, call me Rob."

Stub Martin and Larry Fowler came over next and introduced themselves before introducing the other men drinking coffee.

"Awful glad to see you took your signs down. A lot of these boys hunt and they appreciate you still allowing them to hunt on your farm."

"You should come and train dogs with us sometime," said Larry. "Stub and I train our bird dogs a couple afternoons each week."

"Sounds like fun, but I know nothing about dogs or how to train them."

"Stub thinks he is a brilliant trainer, but the rest of us think the dog knows more than the owner."

"We are training this afternoon. Why don't you come along and see what this bird dog business is all about?"

They arranged for a time and place to meet and the other locals smiled and wished him a good day.

Robert left the restaurant with a skip in his step and couldn't wait for the afternoon session to arrive so he could see first-hand what a bird dog training session was about.

Robert met his new acquaintances at four o'clock. Stub and Larry already had their two dogs out of their cages. The German short haired pointer belonged to Stub and the chocolate lab was Larry's.

The dogs were sleek and fit and in perpetual motion.

Both men had training dummies which they threw for the dogs to retrieve. The dogs would sprint out on command, pick up the canvas dummy, race back, sit by their master and gently release the dummy into the trainer's hand.

"Here, you throw one," said Stub.

Robert lofted the dummy in the air and waited for the dog to race out and retrieve it, but the dog never moved.

Stub whispered in Robert's ear, "The dog won't retrieve until you say, fetch."

When Robert gave the command to fetch, the dog was off like a rocket, picked up the dummy, came back and sat by Robert's side before releasing the dummy into Robert's hand.

Robert went home after the hour-long training session, fired up his computer, and started learning as much as he could about bird dogs.

After several weeks of extensive research, Robert finally became convinced that the dog for him would be an English Springer Spaniel. Through his research he learned that English Springer Spaniels have great personalities, make good house dogs, are flush dogs rather than the rangy pointers. The Springer Spaniel would suit him better on his farm which was made up of small pockets of timber and grassland.

Robert studied blood lines extensively and finally settled on a four-month-old Springer. The hefty price tag of $4,000 didn't bother him in the least, but he never mentioned the price to Larry or Stub for fear of offending them.

He drove to the Madison airport to pick up the spaniel. As soon as the wiggling pup was out of his cage it was love at first sight. The pup came bounding out of his crate and immediately began licking Robert's face, his tail going a million miles an hour. Robert had packed some puppy chow and drinking water before loading the pup into the front seat of the pickup. After licking Robert's hands, the pup curled up in the front seat and went to sleep.

I'm home, thought Robert, as a quiet peace fell over him.

Robert didn't object when the puppy chewed on the furniture, nor did he mind the potty training when pools of urine suddenly appeared on the floor. All this would be handled in time. He found joy each morning when the pup would clamber up in bed with him, licking him with its raspy tongue until Robert got up and let the pup out to play. The pup chased everything in sight and that is how he finally got his name.

"I'm going to name you Chase," Robert said, "because all you want to do is chase everything you see."

The double entendre with the name was not lost on Robert.

Robert continued to train with Stub and Larry, learning much about bird dogs and their habits. He sometimes even taught some training technique he had researched on the internet to his two best friends.

He further entrenched his standing in the community on advice from Betty Flanders. He set up a free tax preparation service on Thursday mornings. He never accepted money for his work, and he helped the town's citizens save money through tax loopholes and deductions which he used to provide to millionaires who had paid exorbitant fees for his expertise. Robert would bring Chase with him on Thursday mornings and the dog would curl up at his feet.

As time passed, he established two scholarships at the local high school. The valedictorian and salutatorian would each be given $10,000 scholarships to help defray the cost of post high school education. He did this anonymously, but the townspeople all knew where the money was coming from. He built wooden fences on his property and planted wild grasses to provide cover for the quail, ruffed grouse and pheasants.

Robert had never been happier. Happiness, he decided, wasn't about money. Happiness was helping the townspeople who had welcomed him with open arms once he learned about the culture of small towns. Love, on the other hand, was having Chase by his side every day.

He hunted birds with a British .20-gauge shotgun that had cost him $7,000, almost twice what he had paid for Chase. How silly, he thought, the gun was a beautiful piece of craftsmanship with meticulous engraving on the barrel. The stock of the gun had the finest inlaid wood. But Chase had brought him something that was priceless. Chase had brought him peace, tranquility and love.

Each year he spent $5,000 at a pheasant farm and had the birds released on his land, some each month, so the local hunters would have an abundance of birds to hunt. When asked where all the pheasants came from, he would shrug and say, "It must have been a banner hatch this year."

After 25 years, he eventually moved into town after having hip replacement surgery. He still went to the restaurant each morning to see his buddies, swap stories, and drink coffee.

He awoke one crisp fall morning feeling good. He called for Chase and scratched the dog behind the ears.

"What do you think old boy, do you have one more hunt in you before the weather turns cold? I'd like to go back to the farm. Maybe we could scare up a grouse or a pheasant. Just one last hunt together, Chase. Are you up for it?"

Robert pulled on his hunting pants and boots. The hunting jacket was made with extra pouches to store any birds that he might shoot. He took three bottles of water and put them in his jacket as well. He backed his pickup out of the garage, loaded the dog in the front seat of the pickup and drove out to the edge of the farm.

"Come on Chase. I've done my job. I've got my .20 gauge. It's up to you to find the birds."

Robert walked slowly, careful to not put too much pressure on his surgically repaired hip.

The sun was burning off the last dregs of morning fog and the trees were dressed in their finest fall colors, a tapestry of red, yellow, and orange.

They hunted for over an hour with nothing to show for it except the indescribable beauty of the driftless area.

Robert removed his hunting hat and wiped beads of perspiration from his brow.

"Come, Chase. Let's cross the stream. We both need a cool drink of water."

The dog went to lap up water and Robert settled in at the trunk of a gnarled white oak.

He took out one of the bottles from his jacket and took a deep gulp. It felt good to have a rest and watch the leaves settle down around him. Two squirrels played in an adjacent tree unaware of the human beneath them.

"Give me another minute Chase, and we will finish the hunt."

"I just need a few more minutes to rest and then I'll be ready to go."

My God, he thought, does anything get any better than this, sitting under a tree and watching the splendor of autumn unfold before you?

He took one last look at nature's glory as a leaf lifted from its mooring and sailed into the breeze.

"Okay, Chase, I promise, just one more minute of rest and I'll be ready."

The next morning Stub Martin and Larry Fowler were drinking coffee when Stub asked Larry if he had seen Robert lately.

"No, come to think of it he hasn't been in for a while."

Stub shuffled his feet and looked down at the floor before blurting out, "There is something wrong with Robert."

"What the hell do you mean there is something wrong with Robert?"

"Well, he was in here last week and he had his old pickup and his young dog Molly with him."

When he was ready to leave, he said, "Come on, Chase, get up in the cab."

"Hell," said Stub, "Chase has been dead for ten years."

"It took Robert years to get over losing Chase."

"What is Molly, eight or nine months old?"

"Look," said Larry, "it was probably just a slip of the tongue."

"Here is another thing I heard recently," said Stub.

"Two townspeople recently told me that their taxes were done incorrectly. One of them is looking at a small fine and the other taxes were filed late."

"Damn it Stub, what the hell are you saying. Robert is the smartest man either one of us has ever known."

Stub looked down at his feet, looking for an answer that wasn't there, before looking his friend in the eye. "What I'm saying is, the elevator doesn't go all the way to the top anymore. Robert has had lapses in memory recently, you just haven't noticed."

Larry looked at his friend for a moment before saying, "Okay, get in my car. We are taking a ride over to Robert's house right now."

The first thing they noticed when they arrived at Robert's house was the garage door. The garage was open, Roberts pickup was gone, and there was no sign of Molly.

"Okay," said Larry, "now you've got me worried. We are going out to the farm."

They arrived at the farm and saw Robert's pickup in his regular parking space. They checked the hood of the car, but the engine was cold.

They set off on a fast pace, stopped every few minutes to call out for Robert.

They went on, calling to their friend every few minutes. Suddenly they saw Molly as she came bounding out of the woods.

It took them another ten minutes to find Robert. He was still sitting upright against the oak tree. One look told them they didn't have to check to see if he was breathing.

They gently removed the .20-gauge shotgun and

checked the chamber. The chamber was empty, and a smell test told them the gun had not been fired recently.

Larry called the two member police department with the terrible news about Robert and the police then notified the mortuary to come and collect Robert's body.

Both Stub and Larry were emotionally spent. Larry took Molly home with him and fed and watered her.

Word in small towns travels fast and before the sun had set everyone within ten miles had been informed of Robert's passing.

The police called Robert's only brother with the sad news and he promised to catch the first available flight out to Madison. He told the police that he would rent a vehicle and drive out from the airport.

Larry and Stub met Robert's younger brother Jeremy at the mortuary, and both noticed the physical similarity between the two men. Jeremy said he would stay on after the funeral to close the house and remain until the will was read.

The Courier Press carried the obituary in their weekly paper which sold out within the day. It carried the usual information on Robert's age, where he attended universities and his various degrees. The news that shocked everyone in the town was notification of his full name, Robert Chase Miller. His deceased wife's name was Molly Miller.

The visitation lasted well past the listed time. Everyone in the town came, each with a story of Robert's kindness. Betty Flanders, always the one with the quick wit and a ready joke, cried so hard she had to be helped from the funeral home.

Robert was buried on a Monday afternoon at his farm. It was a beautiful fall day with the sun shining through on the golden leaves of maple trees. He was buried adjacent to the grave of Chase, united once again, forever.

As the mourners were leaving the grave site, there was a rustle of grass near the grave. A pheasant erupted from its hiding place nearby, rose in the sky, set its wings, and sailed off into the setting sun.

Robert's last will and testament was read a week later. He had set aside enough money to make sure the school could fund the scholarships on the interest that would accrue each year. His endowment would fund the purchase of pheasants each autumn. He had placed the farm in a charitable foundation allowing everyone access to the land for walking and hunting purposes. Larry and Stub were appointed executors.

The .20-gauge shotgun was bequeathed in the will to Larry Fowler and Stub with a hand-written note from Robert. The note read:"I bequeath my shotgun to Stub Martin and Larry Fowler in the hope they might shoot a bird out of the sky rather than just shooting holes in the sky."

Before he flew back east, Jeremy had one last request. He asked if Stub and Larry would adopt Molly. His apartment complex did not allow dogs and he knew this is where Robert would want Molly to stay. Stub and Larry graciously accepted the offer.

Betty Flanders started a fund-raising campaign to erect a monument on the farm. Everyone in town gladly gave something, even if it was only a few dollars.

On a cold December day, a small contingent

gathered and placed the granite monument near the two graves. The inscription on the monument read: "No finer man ever walked these woods and fields than Robert Chase Miller. He was generous to all, giving tirelessly of his time and resources. Because of his generosity, this land shall forever be made available to all sportsmen and visitors. He loved the driftless area, his adopted town, and all its citizens. Most of all, he loved his dogs."

A DAY ALL GEESE WOULD DIE

Plants and animals are always going through stages of vicissitude. We, as humans, go through different stages of change as we transcend from childhood to adolescence, and finally to adulthood. Eventually we grow old and feeble, lose our ability to function bodily or mentally, then pass through the last stage of vicissitude when we die. Changes in our life can happen rapidly or at a snail's pace. Most of the time we are not even aware of those changes taking place.

Kurt Kinder and his two grown sons, Matt and Jeff, would not have known what vicissitude was, nor would they have cared, as they launched their sixteen-foot flat bottom Monarch boat into the Mississippi River in a late November morning. Their 25 horse *Evinrude* outboard motor would serve them well as they headed downriver to their favorite location to hunt ducks. Their gas tank, was full and the *Evinrude* motor had just been overhauled. They had made plans to spend the whole day hunting unless they were lucky enough to fill their bag limit early.

Kurt had moved his family to a small town on the Upper Mississippi River Flyway when the boys were eight and ten years old. He and his wife, Alice, wanted to move to a small town where their boys could grow up and participate in sports and learn to hunt and fish in the Driftless Area of Wisconsin. Once they made the move, they never had a day's regret about their decision. The small town they ended up moving to was welcoming, and the boys adjusted well to a new school system.

One of the first lessons they learned was nearly everyone who lived in the area was either a hunter or a fisherman. Most folks were both. Kurt joined the town's Rod and Gun Club where he learned how to shoot a shotgun and a deer rifle. The boys started out fishing with cane poles and migrated up to spinning rods and reels shortly thereafter. Kurt allowed the boys to join the Rod and Gun Club when they became teenagers.

They were all interested in learning as much as they could about the Driftless Area, and the Mississippi River Basin was a great incubator for their curiosity. They swam and fished in the local ponds, and as teens trapped muskrats, mink and raccoon to earn some extra spending money. They learned to hunt for Ginseng along the steep slopes of the surrounding hills in the fall, looking for the telltale red berries. This added even more spending money to their coffers. They used the money to buy used shotguns from a local gas station, slash, sporting goods store. They bought the shells to hunt ducks from the same store.

Kurt bought a reloading kit to save money on shells so all three picked up their spent shells, stuck them in their coat pockets and spent one evening a week reloading the shells. The whole family was frugal in that way. "Waste Not, Want Not" became the family motto.

The river was their teacher and they were eager students. They learned to identify freshwater plants like water lilies, gray headed cone flowers, bulrushes, cattail as well as the free-floating plants like duck weed, stone wart and ostrich ferns. When they looked in the brownish water of the Mississippi River, they saw greenish free-floating algae, plankton without stems, as well as cardinal flowers and mosses that waved in the rivers current.

From their science class in school they were taught something about the 325 species of birds that live along the upper Mississippi River Flyway. They learned that forty percent of all waterfowl migrate along the Mississippi River. They taught themselves to recognize hawks, turkeys, peregrine falcons, eagles, great blue herons, cormorants, and turkey vultures.

They learned that 119 species of fish swam in the Upper Mississippi River Basin. There were walleye pike, saugers, channel catfish, northern pike, bluegill, perch and crappie. By the time the boys were in high school, they had caught many of these species.

They learned that peat bogs in Minnesota could be as deep as ten feet. There was an abundance of marshes that dotted the entire region and Tamarack forests in Minnesota and northern Wisconsin. As the Mississippi River snaked through the Driftless Area of Wisconsin, Minnesota, and Iowa you couldn't help noticing the islands that dotted the backwater of the river. There were small ponds and potholes where frogs, snakes, turtles, mink, and muskrat lived. Fox and mink roamed the shoreline looking for an easy meal of dead fish. If you were especially lucky, they might spot an otter family, making small chittering sounds as they spent the day playing and chasing fish for their lunch. The smaller animals were prey to the hawks, owls, and eagles that glided overhead as they looked for movement below. If an animal had died, it wouldn't take long before turkey vultures showed up gliding in smaller and smaller concentric circles until eventually landing and feasting on the dead. There was life, death, and play on the river and as time passed the Kinder men became acquainted with each of those phenomena.

Those lessons were on display as the Kinder men pushed off from the boat landing. They had gone to bed early before rising in darkness. Few words were spoken as they rubbed their sleepy eyes. They dressed quickly and packed well. They layered their clothing, and each had a large thermos of steaming coffee to take off the morning chill. They brought along a plentiful supply of sandwiches and snacks, for times when hunger pangs reminded them it was time to eat. They had hooded jackets and mittens and hip boots with two heavy pairs of wool socks to keep their feet warm.

The last thing that got loaded into the boat were

their two Labrador retrievers, Molly and Jake. They had bought them when they were pups and through trial and error had taught them to become first class bird dogs. The dogs would sit patiently in the blind, shivering as they scanned the horizon for birds on the fly.

The weather was decent for a mid-November day. It had been 38 degrees when they left their houses with only a slight breeze out of the north. The Evinrude turned over on the first pull and the boat created a small wake into gentle waves as they turned the boat downstream. Fifteen minutes later they cut the motor and drifted into a small landing area on a section of sandy beach.

The dogs got out first to do their duty and the men followed suit. They didn't uncase their guns. There would be plenty of time for that once they got to the narrow peninsula where they would set up blinds that would hide them from approaching ducks. They walked through old forest growth of river birch, bur oak, green ash, hackberry, cottonwood trees and white oak. The silver maple leaves caught the slight breeze, turning on their sides and showing their silver color.

It took the hunters ten minutes of steady walking to reach the Peninsula. They saw deer tracks and noticed where beaver had recently toppled a small sapling and dragged it off. The sapling would become part of a feed bed, food for the colony of beaver when ice covered the river.

Little voles scurried through yellow grass to hide as the hunters passed by. Life was everywhere if you knew where to look and took your time to stop and listen. A hoot owl stood erect in a tree and watched as the hunters passed beneath the tree it was perched in. When the hunters were directly under the tree, the owl took flight. The sound of beating wings was all the hunters heard as the owl flew toward a distant tree.

The Peninsula they were to hunt on jutted out into a backwater lake. There were willows on the Peninsula and tall reeds that had turned a yellowish brown. The lake was shallow, no more than three feet deep where they were going to set up their hunting blinds. There was an abundance of lily pads that had been bright green in spring, but now were dull with mottled brown spots. When the breeze would pick up, some of the lily pads would flip over and then right themselves, as water droplets ran across the pads and draining back into the lake before settling down. The pods on top of the lily pads contained the seeds for next year's crop. Eventually the lily pads would shrivel and sink, the seeds would become embedded in the bottom on the shallow lake and new pads would sprout and grow in the spring.

The three Kinder men spread out about twenty yards apart, each staking their claim to a small piece of earth. They cleared off a spot a couple of yards long, tromping down grass and reeds. They left enough tall reeds for cover, their own little killing zone, a place to hide until ducks came into range.

The sky was just turning a brilliant pink in the east. The sun slowly rose into the sky, a chariot determining its own pace of ascent and descent. It would be another thirty minutes before the sun would be up in all its glory, but the hunters would be ready when ducks started to arrive for their morning feed.

The two Labrador retrievers sat near their masters,

heads pointing skyward. The hunters took their cue from the dogs whose eyesight was much keener than any humans. When the dog's tails began to wag, when they rose off their haunches, the hunters knew the dogs had spotted ducks. The hunters followed the direction of the dogs until they too saw the first ducks of the morning.

Each of the Kinder men had learned how to use a duck call. They would practice together and separately as the season opener approached. There was a little competition at stake to see which Kinder man was the most proficient with a duck call, but the competition seldom ended with a declared winner.

Kurt was the only Kinder who ever bothered to tote along a goose call. In all the years they had hunted together, none of the Kinder men had shot a goose. Sure, they had all heard geese honking as they flew high overhead. They thought that next to the howl of a wolf, nothing sounded as wild as the honking of a flock of geese. Every time you looked skyward and heard the honking of geese the sound always sent shivers down your spine.

It wasn't that Canadian Geese didn't use the Upper Mississippi River Flyway because they did. The flyway was their route to the southern states where the geese stayed until spring. You might see them in a farmer's cornfield as they searched for kernels of corn the pickers had missed. You would hear them on the river, but they always seemed to be flying high, out of shotgun range. You would watch them as they flew in perfect symmetry heading south.

The shooting started slowly in the morning and tapered off quickly. By noon they had shot two teal, a wood duck, and one mallard. They had hit two other ducks who flinched in mid-air, set their wings and sailed over the forested area out of sight. The dogs had worked admirably, and they hadn't lost any of the ducks that splashed down in the lake.

They ate their lunches, threw the crusts of bread to the hungry retrievers, and drank their coffee. They discussed how much longer they wanted to hunt with no definitive answer. None of them wanted to be the first to say, "Maybe it is time to head on home."

They squatted and waited as water from their boot prints seeped through the dry grass.

At three o'clock in the afternoon the sky was dead still. By three fifteen clouds rolled in over the eastern horizon, and the temperature dropped precipitously. Sleet soon began to pelt them until they had no choice but to pull on their rain slickers. They were just about to call it a day when they heard the geese. At first it was a faint sound just above the sound of the rain and sleet. All the Kinder men seemed to hear the geese at the same time. They started to scan the horizon as the honking got closer and louder. They spotted the geese a minute later. The dogs were on high alert following the flight of the descending birds. The geese seemed to hang in the sky as if in a portrait looking for a secluded place to land. The peninsula, with the timber background helped block a good deal of the wind and the shallow lake remained relatively calm. This seclusion of the lake did not go unnoticed by the geese as they fought the wind, set their wings and started a glide pattern toward the hunters and the waiting dogs.

Kurt reached in his coat and pulled out his goose

call. He put the call to his lips and began calling.

There was no time for the Kinder men to separate. They would stand together and either all of them would get shooting or none of them would. At first it appeared that the geese would not respond to the call but soon they set a path directly toward the hunters. They were honking frantically ready to set down in calmer waters. They set their wings and started to glide toward the waiting hunters, no more than twenty meters off the water. Matt was the first to rise from his crouch and shoot the lead goose. The goose somersaulted in mid-air and tumbled into the shallow water.

Jeff stood alongside his brother and shot a goose who was back peddling its wings in a vain attempt to regain altitude. Jeff broke the wing of the goose and the bird tumbled from the sky. Kurt shot next and managed to down his bird as the flock broke for cover and gained altitude. The flock turned and headed back into the storm.

Both dogs broke for the downed geese. Jake got to the first goose that had been shot. The goose was dead, and Jake had an easy retrieve.

Molly broke for the goose with the broken wing. Things went okay until she got to the goose. The goose, very much alive, began beating Molly on her head with her good wing. Molly was forced to circle the goose until Jake got there, grabbed the goose by the neck and carried it back to shore. Jeff picked up the goose and quickly rung its neck until the goose was dead.

Molly leaped back into the water and dragged the third goose which was dead back to shore.

The Kinder men had each killed their first goose. They were overjoyed with their success when the flock of geese turned on the wind and returned to search for their fallen mates. The Kinder men closed rank, raised their shotguns, and watched as the geese came in low over the water, turning their heads from side to side desperately looking for members of the flock. All three Kinder men shot at the same time and three more geese fell into the shallow water.

The flock once again gained altitude and flew over the island forest. Jake and Molly did an admirable job of retrieving and three more geese joined the growing pile near the hunter's feet.

The Kinder men all looked at each other and couldn't believe their luck. Six geese in one day left them speechless.

They looked at the pile of geese, commended the dogs on their good work, congratulating each other on their marksmanship when the flock once again returned. They barely had time to reload when the geese were upon them honking for the downed birds. This time both Kurt and Jeff downed two birds. The flock whirled in mid-air and flew away over the timber. The hunters waited fifteen minutes before deciding the geese would not be returning.

They loaded everything into their boat and fought high waves on their way back to the boat landing. They were wet and tired, but they couldn't wait to get home with their geese. There were three other hunting parties at the boat landing when they shut off the motor and glided to a stop. Hunters are always interested in others who have had success. As soon as the geese were spotted, every other hunter quickly gathered around to look at the geese and talk about the hunt.

"Where were you hunting?"

"How many geese do you have?

"Damn, nine geese, really?"

"That's a hell of a hunt."

"Never saw that many geese killed on the flyway before."

"How did your dog's work with birds that big?"

"Bet you will never have another hunt like that in your lifetime."

"Wish I had been there to see it."

"You say the geese just kept circling and returning. I've heard they will do that, but I've never seen it."

The questions went on and on until the other hunters started to slowly drift away. The fellow hunters never mentioned how many ducks they had bagged on their outing. The day belonged to the Kinders. No other stories could compare to the sight of nine dead geese in the bow of the boat.

The other hunters said, "Congratulations on the kill," loaded up their boats, and went on their way.

When the Kinder men got home, they shared the good news of their hunt. Mrs. Kinder took out the family camera and snapped photos with each of her men posing with the geese.

"Okay," she said. "You shot them; you get to clean them."

The men got out three large garbage bags and started to pluck feathers. The plucking took longer than anyone expected, and they still hadn't gutted the birds. There were feathers all over the yard which brought more neighbors out of their houses to see what was going on. It was eight o'clock at night by the time they finished gutting the birds. They kept one goose out to eat and put the rest in their big freezer.

Since none of the Kinder family had ever eaten a goose before they were all looking forward to a feast the following night.

Alice Kinder was up the next morning researching how to prepare a goose for cooking. It looked pretty much like cooking a turkey. You baste the bird, add seasoning, add stuffing if so inclined and stick the bird in the oven. She put the goose in the oven at three o'clock and started preparing the rest of the feast.

The table was set with salad, homemade bread, mashed potatoes, peas and gravy, as well as two different kind of pies. The aroma of the goose permeated the kitchen. It came out of the oven at six o'clock and Kurt set about carving the goose, putting it on the table by six thirty.

The family loaded up their plates and everyone started to eat. Jeff took a hearty bite of the goose and began to chew with enthusiasm. His face started to turn red just about the time everyone else took their first bites of the bird.

"Damn," he said, "that has to be the worst tasting meat I have ever eaten." He got up from the table, went outside and spit everything out. Within minutes everyone else scurried out and joined in the process of spitting out the meal they had looked forward to having.

"Tastes awful," said Kurt. "Can't eat that stuff. Didn't know anything could taste that bad."

"Don't ask me to ever cook another goose," said Alice.

"What the hell do we do with the other eight geese?" said Matt.

"Gabe Jenkins has coon hounds. They will eat anything. Let's load up the geese and take them over to his place."

They loaded the cooked goose and the eight frozen geese into their truck and took them over to Gabe's house, and offered up the geese for dog food. Gabe took a hatchet and split the geese into smaller pieces. Gabe tossed a chunk of goose to each of his coon dogs. The hounds smelled the geese for a few seconds before happily gobbling down the proffered meat.

"Could have told ya, if youda asked," said Gabe. "Goose is damn poor eatin', but my hounds like 'em fine. Those geese will feed my hounds for a couple of weeks."

The Kinder men continued to hunt ducks for many more years, but they never had the chance to shoot another goose. They were left with some well-worn photographs that had been framed and put on the family mantel. Those framed photos showed the smiling Kinder men holding up nine dead geese. Every time they looked at the photos, it brought back memories of that fateful day when a flock of geese kept circling, returning for the fallen flock.

It was a fateful day for both geese and men. It was a day when three hunters would prevail, and a day when all geese would die.

THE LAST SEASON

The old man sat at his fly-tying vice. He was just finishing tying an elk hair caddis trout fly. He looked at the fly he was tying and then at the four others that he had already finished. He glanced over at the four flies and wasn't satisfied in what he saw. Once, in years past, he had tied perfection. Now all he saw were the imperfections. Thank goodness trout aren't concerned with perfection, he thought. He knew that presentation of a well-cast fly upon the water was more important that the quality of the fly being cast. Trout will eat almost anything that is presented in a way that that seems natural. He had watched countless trout fishermen cast their lines with expensive equipment and fly boxes containing hundreds of flies. Many of them would spend five minutes trying to select the perfect fly. They would tie the selected fly on the tippet of their fly line, cast the fly like they were throwing a grenade, creating such a splash that any trout in the vicinity would immediately dash for cover. After a few minutes of fruitless casting, they would select another fly and repeat the same process. If they had cast the fly over the water and let it gently touch down creating a natural presentation, they would have caught the trout with their first cast.

He had learned at a young age that the first cast is always the most important cast. It is preferable to take your time, look at the how the water flows, and then make your first cast count. A brown trout is by nature a sprinter. It can reach maximum speed in two-tenths of a second. Once a trout is spooked you've lost that trout before you have even hooked it. Cast your line above the trout, allow for a natural drift, mend the line if you must, keep the excess line sliding through your fingers and wait for the strike.

The old man thought of all these things as he sat at his tying vice. The trembling in his hands had started a few years ago, and if he were honest with himself, had only gotten worse with the passage of time. When he was younger, he tied lots of different fly patterns. As he perfected his skill over many years, he relied more and more on a few tried-and-true patterns. The size of the pattern you tied was equally important. Generally, smaller was better when it came to a trout fly.

He relied on flies that had caught trout a hundred years ago and still caught most of the trout today. How could you go wrong with an Adams, an elk hair caddis, a prince nymph, a blue winged olive, a pheasant tail, or a hare's ear. They had passed the test of time, caught trout in the West and the Mid-West.

They had caught trout in big rivers and small streams, in valleys and in mountain lakes. Why mess with hundreds of patterns when true perfection had already been tied many years ago.

It had taken him a lifetime to learn all these lessons. He tried to remind himself that he had been young once and had made countless mistakes before becoming truly proficient. There had been no one to teach him how to cast a line or how to feel the tug when the back cast went taut. No one had taught him how to read the water and follow the seam that carried the insects to the trout. No one to show him how to cast the fly line over the water and not on the water, allowing the fly to settle naturally with a kiss as light as a butterfly's wings.

Mother nature had graded him hard, but fair. He had seen many novice fly fishermen give up, but that had never deterred him. If anything, it had inspired him. When he was on a trout stream, he was always in a beautiful place. The water was clean, fast moving, and undulating. The stream was a moving entity that contained untold millions of living entities. All he ever had to do was pick up a rock from the bottom of a stream, turn it over, and see the underwater life stages of nymphs. Caddis larvae, damsel flies, stone flies, mosquitoes, mayflies and midges were there for all to see if they just took the time to look.

He had gleaned that information of aquatic life in a lifetime of fishing. Ice cold water had slowly turned his fingers arthritic. It was the price you paid for doing something you loved. He had torn tendons in his ankles that had shelved him for months at a time, but once recovered, he always came back to the streams.

He had rotator cuff surgery a few years ago, timing the surgery for the day after the trout season ended. As injuries mounted and age became an issue, he needed more time to recuperate and prepare for the upcoming season.

Trout have a brain the size of a pea, but they continue to confound you all the days of your life. No matter how much you learn about trout, there are days when they still confuse you. Some days they can be voracious in their attack, while other days they might turn on a fly, but never take it. Instead of frustrating you, they entice you. They make you want to learn more about these beautiful fish. You could spend your whole life learning about the habits of trout and still feel like there were more lessons to be learned.

He thought of these things as he took off his tying glasses, rubbed his tired eyes and placed the last caddis fly with the others he had tied. He would soak these flies in a waterproofing solution to assure they floated higher and lasted longer. Eventually they would become water-logged and you would need to add more fly floatant.

He turned off the overhead light and gingerly rose out of his chair. He stood for a moment to stretch his back before slowly climbing the five steps from the basement to a hallway that led to his living room. He poured himself a cup of cold coffee that had been made this morning and put it in the microwave to reheat. He sat in his easy chair, turned on the television to a news channel and sipped his coffee. The news was too depressing, too many wars, too much national debt, too many politicians trying to hold onto their seats in Congress without a thought of what was best for their constituents. He only watched the news channel a few minutes before turning off the television. Why the hell don't they have term limits, he thought.

He sat in the dark thinking about the decision he had made more than a month ago. Even the easy chair couldn't ease the pain in his hips anymore. He took too many pills to take the edge off, but they all had some unpleasant side effects. Allopurinol for gout, a Statin for high cholesterol, a baby aspirin to ward off a possible heart attack, a series of vitamins, and Warfarin as a blood thinner.

It was now the early days of May. He had missed the early trout season when snow was a white carpet that blanketed the ground. He had gotten a cold in March that hung on longer than it should have. The cold had left him weak, his knees hurt, and his hips weren't getting any better. So, after long deliberation he decided that this would be his last season of trout fishing. He had waited until after the start of the season before coming to his final decision. It wasn't a decision he wanted to make, but he knew it was a decision he had to make. He could no longer take the cold weather in March. Putting his hands in water that hovered around forty degrees made his finger so numb it was hard to tie on a fly. It was those realizations that finally convinced him his days as a trout fisherman were coming to an end.

He had a daughter that lived in Florida who insisted he come live with her. He knew that was the right thing to do, but still the thought depressed him. He could still fish, she said, they would just be a different kind of fish.

He arose the next day and quickly looked at the

temperature. The forecast was for highs in the mid-60's with overcast skies and a slight breeze. Today, he decided, would be his first outing of his final season. He knew he'd be lucky to make it out on a trout stream more than a dozen times, but today was a good day so he put that thought out of his mind.

He had so many memories floating through his head as he prepared to leave his house. In his lifetime he had seen presidents come and go. Some in grace, some in disgrace, and some in coffins. He had raised one daughter and no sons. There would be no son to follow him down to the stream he would be fishing today. There would be no companion to see the beauty of a trout rising to a dry fly. No one to watch a hatch of countless insects rising off the water. No one to teach the cycle of the fishing year. First there were tiny nymphs sunk down with weight in deep quiet pools to entice slow moving trout. Next came small dry flies, then larger nymphs, that gave way to larger dry flies. He used streamers in early autumn to entice larger trout. Finally, he would use smaller dry flies as midge hatches came off the water to end the season. The season would often start and end with blue wing olives. They would be there in March as the snow started to melt, go away as summer progressed, but return in autumn as leaves fell on the water.

He had tied all those flies in his younger years when the snow was three feet deep as he prepared for the cycle of the upcoming season. All that was left now were the memories of how he used to prepare. Everything else would be left behind.

He had carefully chosen the stream he would fish today. The stream ran through a long meadow. The walking would be easier, and he might not have to get in and out of water as often. He had already missed the early season when the weather wasn't good. He didn't miss the cold, the slippery banks, the ground with frost seeping out, hard one minute, slippery the next. He didn't miss ice in small puddles.

He had waited all winter for this warm spring day. He loaded up his car, put his gear in the back seat, double-checked everything to make sure he had not left anything behind. It took him twenty minutes to drive to the stream. He felt lucky when he didn't see another vehicle parked near the stream. It took him another twenty minutes to get his gear on. He slowly threaded the leader through the guides on his fly rod. His final preparation was to tie on one of the caddis flies he had made the night before.

He headed off to the stream with a smile on his face. He could hear the stream gurgling, water cascading over rocks, calling to him. He smiled at the overcast skies, a friend of all trout fishermen. When he reached the first pool, he saw a trout rise, then another. He looked closer and saw caddis flies drying their wings as they floated by on the current, some already lifting off the water and their flight away.

He stripped line from the reel, took several false casts, as he thought to himself, make the first cast count.

ABOUT THE AUTHOR

Harlan Flick was born and raised in De Soto, Wisconsin. He is a graduate of the University of Wisconsin-Platteville. His life has been spent as an educator teaching in public schools in Fennimore, Waunakee, Prairie du Chien and Richland Center, Wisconsin. He then broadened his horizons with teaching stints at international schools in Jakarta, Indonesia for 16 years and Suzhou, China for 3 years.

His overseas experience has taken him to more than 25 countries and allowed many opportunities to travel. The people he met along the way and his diverse experiences have helped shape his view of the world and created in him a greater appreciation of the beauty that is the Driftless Area of Southwest Wisconsin."

Harlan's previous books are *Coins in a Half-Filled Jar, Big River Run Long,* and *One Last Dance With The Dani Tribe.*

He may be reached via email at phflick@gmail.com

Made in the USA
Monee, IL
25 May 2021